MAN HUNGRY

A NOVEL BY

ALAN
MARSHALL

BLACKBIRD BOOKS
NEW YORK • LOS ANGELES

A Blackbird Classic, October 2012

Copyright © 1959 by Alan Marshall

Manufactured in the United States of America.

Cataloging-in-Publication Data

Marshall, Alan.
Man hungry / Alan Marshall.
p. cm.
1. College students—Sexual behavior—Fiction.
2. College teachers—Fiction 3. College students—Fiction.
4. College teachers as authors—Fiction. I. Title.
PS3573.E9 M36 2012 813'.54—dc22 2012935500

Blackbird Books
www.bbirdbooks.com
email us at editor@bbirdbooks.com

ISBN 978-1-61053-014-9

First Blackbird Edition

10 9 8 7 6 5 4 3 2 1

MAN HUNGRY

PROLOGUE
THREE YEARS AGO

THE ROOM WAS A BOX, small, square, slant-lit by smoky sunlight angling through the ancient, filthy Venetian blinds, stripes of light on the rug, faded, maroon and worn. In the kitchenette, a doorless closet crammed with tiny sink, stove, refrigerator, a hopeful fly buzzed over the pile of dirty dishes in the sink. The Sunday paper, brought three days ago, was scattered throughout the room, on the two sagging armchairs, on the jelly-smeared kitchen table, on the floor. In the corner farthest from the door and nearest to the one window, the cat's dirtbox reeked of ammonia, while the cat herself lay sleeping on the mantelpiece above the bricked-up fireplace.

The girl lay on the sofa bed, still opened out across the room. It was late summer and hot, and the sheets were wrinkled and thick, trailing from the sides and foot of the bed. The girl had propped two pillows behind her head, and was half-sitting, smoking a cigarette and reading typewritten pages of manuscript. She was nude, her body glistening with sweat, her flat stomach rising and falling slightly as she breathed. An ashtray on the sheet beside her was surrounded by tiny flecks of ash. The girl read slowly, methodically, an expression of gloomy concentration on her face.

The man was seated before the card table on the other side of the room. His portable typewriter was on the card table, and he was typing furiously. To the left of the typewriter was a pile of manuscript, pockmarked with pencil corrections. To the right was a small notebook, lying open. Beyond the typewriter, between typewriter and wall, were stacks of bond paper, carbon paper and onion skin. A chair to the man's left held a half-full beer bottle and an empty, stained coffee cup. As he finished a page, he pulled it from the machine, removed the carbon paper from between good copy and onion skin, placed these two on a chair to his right, drank from the beer bottle, reached for fresh paper, put it in the machine, flipped the top sheet of the pencil-corrected manuscript to the growing pile of discarded paper on the floor, and turned the page of the notebook. Then he typed again, the portable chattering like a monkey.

Behind him, the girl grunted, shifted position, and said, "Found another one." He didn't answer. She picked up the ballpoint pen from beside the ashtray, corrected a typographical error on the page she was reading, and dropped the pen back beside the ashtray, where it made another blue smudge on the sheet.

The typing continued. The girl finished the pages she had been reading, and climbed wearily out of bed. It was hot, and muggy, and almost painful to move. She put the read and corrected portion in an open cardboard box, which had originally contained the bond paper, and went to the kitchenette to open another bottle of beer, which she put on the chair beside the man. He said, "Thanks," without looking up. She picked up the portion he had just finished typing, separated bond from onion skin, and brought the good copy back to bed. She adjusted herself on the damp sheets and started to read.

The cat moved on the mantelpiece, sat up and washed her face, first with one paw, then the other. The man typed. The girl read.

The man said, "Ha!" He got to his feet, knocking the chair over behind him. The cat, startled, dove from the mantelpiece and hid under the bed. The man took the last sheet from the typewriter, sorted paper for a minute, and brought the last portion of the manuscript over to the girl. He was grinning. The sweat poured down his face, his T-shirt and khaki trousers were clinging to him, but he looked cool and content. "It's done," he said. "Finished. Complete."

"I'm hot, baby," she said. "Could I have some iced tea?"

"Sure." Reaching down, he grabbed her thigh and squeezed. "It's all done, baby, it's all done."

"Well, let me *read* it, for heaven's sake."

"Right you are." He brushed his hand roughly across the up-tilted nipples of her breasts, and she giggled, looking up at him. "Read fast," he said.

"I will."

He went to the kitchenette and made iced tea. The cat came out from under the bed, hoping the man was preparing food, and twined around his legs, rubbing herself against him and purring heavily. He almost tripped over her when he moved to the refrigerator for ice, and said, "J.J.! Get the hell away from here."

The girl looked over and patted the bed. "Here, J.J." The cat ignored her.

"I'll get rid of him," said the man. He moved to the sink, slowed down by the cat curling between his feet, and turned the cold water on. He held his hand under the faucet, then held it so it dripped water on the cat. The cat bolted for the bed again, and crawled far underneath.

The man made the iced tea and brought it to the bed. The girl took it, said, "Mmmm," and kept on reading. She had only two pages to go.

He got his beer bottle, half-empty again, and brought it over to the bed. He moved ashtray and pen to the floor, brushed the sheet a bit, without doing much good, and sat down beside the girl. He kicked his slippers off and drank from the beer bottle, his head back and the Adam's apple working like a piston in his throat.

"Pen," she said. He gave it to her, watched her change "teh" to "the," and took the pen back when she was finished with it. Hopefully, he dropped it to the floor again.

The beer was gone by the time she finished reading. She clambered from the bed, put the last pages of the manuscript with the rest, and came back to bed. He studied her face, waiting for her to say something, but she stayed silent, and her face was expressionless. "Well?" he said. She lay beside him, on her back, staring at the ceiling, and he leaned over her, resting on his elbow. "Well? What did you think of it?"

"What did *you* think of it?" she asked him.

"Don't be smart-alecky," he told her. Her near leg was raised, the knee bent, and he squeezed the underpart of her thigh. When she said, "Ouch," he released her, but kept his hand resting against her leg. "That was only a sample," he said. "Give me the information I want, or I call the executioner."

"I thought it was fine," she said. She looked at him and smiled, touching his unshaven cheek with her fingertips. "I think you're fine, too."

He leaned forward and kissed her, their lips warm, their faces slick with perspiration where they touched together. Her belly was hot beneath his hand. "It's finished," he whispered. "It's all done."

She turned her head away. "It's too hot."

"Hah!" He twisted violently on the bed, raised to his knees. "It's *finished!*" he shouted. "A celebration!"

"It's too hot," she said again.

"It's never too hot." He leaped and gestured on the bed, pulling off his clothes, and the cat ran out from under the bed and leaped back up on the mantel. She yawned and stretched out on the cool marble of the mantel top, her tail switching slowly back and forth, in vague irritation at the heat.

"Danny," whispered the girl.

"It's finished," he said again, and fell on her. They wrestled on the hot, damp sheets, their bodies oily and warm, and the discomfort was part of the pleasure. They groaned and twisted, their lashing legs kicking the top sheet to the floor, and the cat raced around the room, leaping and churning, her tail whipping back and forth.

The girl clung to the man, arms and legs encircling him, and she whispered, "Danny, I love you, I love you, oh, Danny, I love you."

"It's finished," he whispered.

The sofa bed creaked, their bodies pulsed together, and the girl went suddenly rigid. Her back was arched, buttocks clear of the bed, her mouth was open in a demanding, silent scream, and he hurried, hurried, and stopped.

Until the first coolness of evening filtered through the Venetian blinds, they lay together in the bed, smoking, drinking beer or iced tea, breathing heavily, touching each other's moist body and smiling together. The cat slept on the mantel, still and silent.

Two months later, the girl left him. There was a note: "Danny. You don't love me. All you love is the book. I can't compete with the book, so I'm not going to stay. But you're making a mistake. You can't love that book forever."

He got the note the same day the letter came, telling him the book had been accepted for publication. He held the two letters, looking from one to the other, and smiled. She was right, and it didn't matter. He could find another woman, but there was only the one book.

PART ONE
BLAKE

1

THE CAMPUS WAS NEW AND UGLY. It was two miles from town, out the divided highway that by-passed the town of Winston on its way to New York, three hundred miles distant. Dan Blake, newly-hired Instructor of English, drove toward the campus in his pale green 1949 Ford, hugging the right lane as the newer, longer, chromier cars hurtled by him, ignoring him and Winston and the campus of Monequois College, on their way to The City. Blake envied the drivers of those cars and wished he could tromp on the accelerator and race them all to New York. But he couldn't. If he drove over forty for too long, a couple of pistons would come screaming out, right through the hood. And he'd be out of money before he was halfway to Manhattan anyway.

He slowed to make the turn through the campus gate, and a truck roared by, doing at least seventy. One of its four rear tires threw a pebble at his windshield, leaving another little pockmark. Blake muttered to himself, eased by the ornamental brick gateposts, and drove up the two-lane blacktop road to the main buildings of the campus.

Monequois College, named after an Indian tribe who had never been this far north, was a liberal arts school, part of the state university. The state had an inferiority complex concerning its Education Department. New York and Pennsylvania were both in the same general neighborhood, and both rated much higher in education. Of course, California beat them both, but California was three thousand miles away. Monequois College was the first completed step in a save-face program originating in the state Department of Education. The campus had taken twelve years from drawing board to completion, and work had stopped every time a new architect came along with an even more modern idea. As a result, the campus was expensive, garish and ugly, looking more like an illustration for the cover of a science fiction magazine than a mid-twentieth century college.

Blake followed the blacktop road as it curved to the right, around the chrome, corrugated iron and red brick gymnasium, the blue and yellow paneled, many-windowed student union and snack bar, the flat-roofed, machine shop-pish lab building, and the white and gold pillbox of a theater, to the faculty office building. He parked in the no parking zone directly in front of the main door, and wearily turned off the engine. The Ford was a tired car, and it made him tired to drive it.

He climbed out of the car and looked at the faculty building. It was another machine shop, very similar to the lab building. It had an overhanging flat roof, that jutted out beyond the walls a good two feet all the way around. It was shaped like a shoebox, made of brick, with wide, short windows lining the upper part of the wall, just under the concrete overhang of the roof. No sunlight in the offices, ever. The architect had probably wanted to keep the hot summer sun from baking the people inside the building, but had forgotten that summer was the only time the school was closed and the offices unused.

The back seat of the Ford was piled high with cardboard cartons. The car was a two-door, and Blake had even more trouble unloading the cartons than he had had loading them at Cape Cod, where he had spent his last summer as a free man, clutching his remaining pennies, making them last until Labor Day. The cartons contained books, all the books he owned, and he had intended to buy a bookcase and keep them in his apartment in the faculty house across the highway from the campus. But then he had seen his office, a tiny cubicle with bookshelves instead of walls, and he knew he would have to fill those bookshelves with something. An English Instructor with empty bookshelves is not an English Instructor hired for a second year.

The cartons weighed a ton, and Blake looked around, hoping to find a Good Samaritan to help him carry them. But the campus seemed absolutely deserted. Class registration was tomorrow, beginning at nine in the morning, and everyone was apparently staying away until the last possible minute. He carried the cartons in himself, one at a time, until they were all in the office, piled on the desk and scattered around on the floor.

He lit a cigarette, draped his sport coat over the swivel chair, removed his tie and hung it on the hook on the back of the door, and went to work transferring his books from the cartons to the shelves. He worked methodically, putting them up in no particular order, thinking about Cape Cod and the letter from the literary agent, saying there would be no need to renew his author's contract, and the last letter from his publisher, signed by an assistant editor he had never heard of before, and telling him that the enclosed royalty check, for seventeen dollars and fifty eight cents, would in all likelihood be the last.

His book was in the third carton. He paused when he saw it, and lifted it tenderly. He held it, touching the illustration on the front of the dust jacket, reading and rereading the title and author. *Drink Deep The Night, by Daniel Blake.* His first book. His last book. Two weeks on the *New York Times* Bestseller List, eleventh place both weeks. Well-received by the critics, who all called it "an unusually fine and perceptive first novel." Just barely enough copies had sold to boost the novel to the bottom of the bestseller list, but that hadn't been enough for either a movie sale or a paperback reprint sale. He had made some money from foreign sales, in Germany and England and, of all places, Brazil, but that had been all.

He had written the book three years ago, when he was twenty four, fresh from Drill University, where he had taken his Master's in American Literature. The book had poured out of him, a first draft in three weeks, the finished product two and a half months later. A faculty member at Drill had introduced him to the literary agent, a woman who worshipped God and Mammon with equal passion. The book had sold to the second publisher who saw it, and Daniel Blake's career had begun.

When had it ended? He had spent the first year relaxing, taking life easy. The book didn't sell enough to finance riotous living, trips to Europe or a garage full of sports cars. But the royalties were large enough to make work unnecessary. So he hadn't worked, at anything, and a year had gone by.

Then he started getting letters from the agent, and letters from the publisher, both wanting to know when he was going to get started on another book. He made promises and he made plans. He unpacked his portable typewriter, set it up on a card table, bought reams of bond paper and onion skin and carbon paper, and filled the refrigerator with beer. He drank the beer and stared at the typewriter, and the letters kept coming from the publisher and the agent.

He did write a second book, finally. It took four months of thinking and four weeks of writing, and the agent sent it back to him, saying it was terrible, he could do better than that.

But he couldn't. He wrote three books during that second year. Two of them were sent back by the agent. The third was sent back by the publisher.

He had signed a two year contract with the agent, self-renewable. But either of them could break the contract at the end of any two year period, merely by writing a letter to the effect that the contract was not to be renewed. The agent wrote such a letter, and Blake phoned long distance to New York to tell the agent what he thought of her. She told him what she thought of him instead. A one-book writer. She was sorry things hadn't worked out better than they had.

He was mad when their conversation ended, mad and afraid. He would show her he wasn't a one-book writer. And he would show himself, while he was at it. He did two more books, and sent them both direct to the publisher. Both came directly back. Then came the last royalty check for

Drink Deep The Night, and the letter signed by a stranger, a sub-editor who had been given the job of brushing Daniel Blake off.

After the binge and the hangover, he started looking for a job. He had enough money to last him through the summer, if he was careful, and then he would have to go to work. He chose teaching because it was the only thing he could think of that he could call himself qualified for. He had an M.A., and he had published a book. Those two facts should be enough to get him a berth in some small college somewhere, where he could draw his pay and have some time to himself.

Monequois College, in the process of expanding from a community college to a full-fledged member of the state university, was looking for an English Instructor to create classes in Composition and Writing. Daniel Blake had filled the bill admirably. He had been hired, at base pay, which is very little in a state-supported college, and had arrived three days before student registration. He had conferred with Doctor Fitzpatrick, head of the English Department, a smug and condescending little man who fancied himself an authority on Chaucer, primarily because he could read Chaucerian English. He had emerged from the conference with four classes of Freshman English and two classes in Creative Writing, Intermediate and Advanced. The next day, the Creative Writing classes had been cut to one, Intermediate, and Advanced would be added the following year.

So here he was. He had moved into his apartment in the faculty building, across the highway. He had bought copies of the Freshman English textbooks from the college bookstore. And now he was filling the shelves of his office with all of his books. They turned out to be not enough. There was still a lot of vacant shelf space. Well, he could take a couple of books out of the library every day for a while, until the shelves were full. As an instructor, he had full library privileges, which meant there was no time limit on books he borrowed.

He stacked the cartons in a corner and sat down at his desk. He felt as though he should write a letter—"Arrived safely. Have moved in. I think I'll probably like it here."—but there wasn't anyone he could think of to write to. His parents were dead, his old friends had faded, and in the annoyed frustration of the last two years, he had made no new friends. He thought back to his own days as an undergraduate, remembering names and faces and unconnected scenes, and he wondered where all those people were today, and if their great ambitions had all foundered just as his had. He hoped they had. He knew it was a petty wish, but he didn't care.

He had left the office door half-open, and now he heard someone coming down the hall. The floor of the building was varnished wood, and footsteps echoed as though the building were a tomb. Blake reached for his tie, then decided the hell with it. He would start being proper tomorrow, for registration.

The footsteps resounded, and then a man appeared, and paused just outside the door, He was tall, well over six feet, with a sharp, narrow face and gray hair chopped short in a squared-off crew cut. He was dressed in a conservative, but rather old, gray suit, with his blue and gray striped tie held to his shirt-front by a small silver tie clasp. The whole dignified effect was shattered by the black loafers on his feet.

The tall man smiled. "New?" he asked.

"Brand new," Blake told him.

"English Department?"

"Does it show that much?"

"No." His smile broadened. "Each department is segregated in here. The offices along this side here are English Department. I'm next door."

Blake got to his feet and extended a hand. "Dan Blake," he said. "Freshman English and Intermediate Creative Writing."

"Roger Kilbride," said the tall man, as they shook hands. "Freshman English, Sophomore English and Drama Workshop."

"We all get Freshman English, I suppose."

"Everyone but Fitzpatrick. It's a detail, like KP in the Army. How many classes do you have?"

"Freshman English? Four."

"Ouch," said Kilbride. "One hundred and twenty themes, every two weeks. Fitzpatrick is really giving you the initiation."

"I know. And I always thought hazing was something done by undergraduates."

"Not at all. They got the idea from their teachers. What was that other class you had?"

"Inermediate Creating Writing. It's new this year."

"Wait a second," said Kilbride. "Dan Blake. Daniel Blake. Are you the Daniel Blake who wrote *Deep Is The Night?*"

"*Drink Deep The Night.* And yes, that was me."

"I remember that book. It was really fine. You never did a second, did you?"

"No. What's this Drama Workshop of yours?"

"The Theatah," said Kilbride, mocking himself. "Acting, directing, set design, anything else I can think of to fill out the semester. The catalog says we put on four plays a semester, but we're lucky to do two a year. You know, we might be able to get together. I've been hoping to be able to do an original one of these days. You start a playwriting class, and my kids will do the plays."

"I can't teach playwriting. I don't know anything about it."

"What difference does that make? I can't teach acting. Our job is to sit around and watch, while the kids find themselves. We set the goals, but they have to figure out how to get there on their own."

"I'm afraid of it, to tell you the truth," said Blake. "I took writing classes myself, when I was in college. As I remember, the stuff we handed the teacher was pretty bad. Now, I'm going to start getting some of it handed to me."

"Freshman English will be good for you. You'll learn how to grade themes without reading them. Are you sticking around here for any special reason?"

"No. I just brought the books in." He waved at the half-full shelves.

"Then let's go get a beer. The opening of school always makes me thirsty."

"I'm with you. Just let me get dressed." Blake put his tie on and shrugged into his coat, then pointed at the empty cartons. "What do I do with those?"

"Just leave them in the hall. The janitor will throw them out."

"Won't he bitch about it?"

"Of course. We'll move them down the hall a ways, and he'll bitch at the Science Department."

They carried the cartons down the hall and left them in the middle of the Science Department's area, then walked out of the building. "My car's right here," said Blake. "I better move it before I get a ticket."

"You've got a faculty sticker, haven't you?"

"Sure."

"Then don't worry. Faculty are gods. We can steal books from the library, park in no parking zones, exceed the campus speed limit and walk on the grass."

"I'm not used to being a member of the power elite yet," said Blake.

Kilbride grinned. "May I ask an impertinent question?"

"Of course."

Kilbride stood by the right-hand door of the Ford and looked across the car top at Blake, over on the driver's side. "Is this job a sinecure for you?" he asked.

"How do you mean?"

"Do you have some burning desire to teach Freshman English and Intermediate Creative Writing?"

"Not exactly. I needed a job, and I didn't have the training to be a truck driver."

"What was it you really wanted to do?"

"Write a second book." Blake ducked his head, to avoid more questions, and climbed into the car.

Kilbride got in beside him. "I thought I recognized a fellow sufferer," he said. "I wasn't asking just to be nosy. I wanted to act. Can I now strain our brand new friendship by giving you some advice?"

"I could probably use some advice."

"Don't blame the kids. It isn't their fault that you're here, nor that I'm here. I am not talking about Freshman English now. That doesn't count. All of the freshmen take it, and all of them hate it. The Natural Science and Social Science kids hate it because it isn't practical. The kids with majors in the Humanities hate it because they already know all the stuff they get in that class. I'm talking about your Writing class. You won't get many kids in that class, and most of the ones you get will be hopeless. But they will be interested, and they will be sincere. And they won't know that they're hopeless. You are a member of the power elite here, all kidding aside, and you can do a hell of a lot of damage if you don't handle these kids right. Take them seriously, at least when they're around. You're the god, but it's their world."

Blake inserted the key in the ignition and jabbed the starter button. He watched his hand as he did so, and said, "Am I that obvious?"

"I'm just remembering me," said Kilbride. "When I first came here, I was going to spend one year. That was all, just one year. I was going to save my money and go back to New York and make it or break it. Do you know how far we are from New York?"

"About three hundred miles, isn't it?"

"More like three million. That first year, I ignored the kids in my classes. I set up the Drama Workshop, the same way you are setting up Intermediate Creative Writing, as a kind of emergency measure, a way to keep my hand in until I got rolling on my career again."

"So what happened?"

"I cheated about fifteen kids. Thirteen or fourteen of them were hopeless and would never have gone anywhere in the theater anyway. One or two of them had possibilities. Those are the ones I cheated."

"Was it fatal?"

"No." Kilbride smiled. "We're not that powerful. One of them transferred to another college the next year. She's in New York now. I see her on television every once in a while, in small parts. She's getting there. I didn't ruin her life. I just wasted a year of it."

"I see."

"It's sometimes tough to tell which ones are hopeless and which ones aren't. So it's best to take them all seriously."

"Maybe I should pack my books again," said Blake. The engine was running, in neutral, complaining the way it always did. "Maybe teaching isn't such a good idea, after all."

"A man who has enough sincerity to write a book like *Drink Deep The Night* has enough sincerity to teach. All you have to do is make teaching a goal, instead of a necessary evil that pays the rent."

"It's time for that beer," said Blake. He shifted into first, and followed the blacktop road on its erratic circuit among the painful and distorted buildings of the campus, back to the highway again. "Which way?"

"To the right."

A wire mesh fence surrounded the campus property. Just beyond the end of the fence along the highway was a small, two-story house that had been converted to a bar and restaurant, named Monequois Inn. The front lawn had been covered with blacktop and turned into a parking lot. Nine or ten cars were already parked there when Blake, following Kilbride's directions turned off the highway and stopped in front of the bar.

Kilbride said, as they were getting out of the Ford, "There was supposed to be no commercial property along the right of way of the highway. I'm told the man who owns this place moved heaven and earth to get permission. It's the only bar close to the campus. If you don't go here, you have to go all the way into town."

"I imagine he does a good business."

"Good enough to warrant two state troopers parked outside seven nights a week."

There were separate doors leading to the bar and restaurant. Kilbride led the way into the bar side of the building, and he and Blake found empty stools at the far end of the long bar stretched down the left-hand wall. It was obviously a college hangout, with pennants on the wall behind the bar, shelves with special mugs, emblazoned with Greek lettering, for regular customers, each of whom had his own private drinking mug, and booths painted and upholstered in maroon and gray, Monequois College's colors. The men's room door had a silhouette of a dog painted on it and, beneath the silhouette, the word, "Pointers." Another dog silhouette was on the ladies' room door, with the word, "Setters," beneath it.

The bar, polished wood, extended the length of one wall, with a row of booths along the other. A doorway beyond the last booth led into the restaurant area. Four of the six booths were occupied, as were all of the barstools, by chattering undergraduates, at a ratio of about three male students for every female. All of the undergraduate girls present were sitting in booths, and all of them seemed to be talking at once. Everyone was telling everyone else about their summer, and no one was taking the trouble to listen.

The overly cute and collegiate decor of the bar, the yakketing undergraduates, the little lecture Kilbride had just delivered, all combined to leave Blake depressed and irritable and weary. He remembered that first year after the book had been published, how good life was, how uncomplicated and pleasant and relaxing, and he wanted that year back again. To get it back, he had to write another book. Good God, he had written *five* more books, trying to get that year back, and all five of them had failed. Shallow, said the agent. Pointless, said the publisher. That was the problem. He wanted that year back. When he'd written the first book, he'd done so because he wanted to write a book. When he'd written the next five, he'd done so because he wanted that year back.

Tomorrow, people would register for Intermediate Creative Writing. What were they hoping for from him? Would any of these chattering, insipid, stupid, annoying children here register for the class? He hoped they wouldn't. He hoped nobody would register. He wondered if he could still withdraw the class, and just teach Freshman English. Kilbride had said that Freshman English didn't count. But he knew he couldn't withdraw Intermediate Creative Writing. That course was what he had been hired for.

Their beer came and they argued good-naturedly about who would pay. Kilbride won, and that meant Blake was to buy the second round.

They drank two beers in silence, full of their own thoughts. Then a girl's voice said, "Doctor Kilbride!" and Blake found himself being introduced to two girls. They were about twenty, both good looking and friendly and dressed in identical tight blue sweaters. Kilbride told him their names, and then suggested they move to a vacant booth, and he was sitting next to the blonde, with the red-head directly across from him. The three of them ignored him for a while, as they talked about school and plays, and he gathered from the conversation that these two were in his Drama Workshop class, both aspiring actresses. The blonde was named Ann and the redhead Harriet.

Blake ordered another round of beer, four this time, and sat back to drink while the other three talked. The booth was narrow, and his hip was touching the well-rounded hip of the blonde girl, Ann. He realized that these two were only about seven years younger than he, and that he would be teaching girls very much like them, eighteen to twenty-one years old, all of them less than ten years his junior. His frustration with his writing had kept him alone, away from women, for a long while now, and suddenly having these two, with their sharply-outlined breasts and their friendly, unsuspicious faces and their tight-skirted hips, so very close to him, was disturbing. He felt nervous and self-conscious, and caught himself staring at the front of Harriet's sweater, wondering if he could get one of these two alone, in the Ford, take her for a ride and have her show him the local Lover's Lane—

No. That would be idiotic. He would find a woman but she would have nothing at all to do with the college. To get caught fooling around with a student would be the worst thing that could possibly happen. It meant loss of reputation, loss of job, and loss of good references. It would finish him as a teacher.

But the sex drive isn't controlled by logic. Both girls were talking rapidly, both of them excited about plans for which play was to be put on that semester, what aspect of theater the class would concentrate on, who would probably get what roles if they chose such and such a play, and their

excitement showed in their bodies. Their breasts moved with
their rapid breathing, and - Ann, sitting beside him, moved
her legs constantly, with nervous excitement, while she
talked. Her near leg rubbed against his, warm and firm, and
he felt color rising in his face. He knew she was unconscious
of the movement, that it wasn't a signal, but he almost took
the chance of signaling back, of returning pressure with
pressure.

He saw Kilbride looking at him, smiling faintly, and he
knew that Kilbride was reading his thoughts again. He wondered if this same thing had happened to Kilbride, that first
year he had been a teacher, and what Kilbride had done
about it. Had he taken some chesty, buxom, excited, trusting
little girl to his apartment in the faculty building, for a private
rehearsal of a scene in some play he was directing? Or had
he resisted the impulse and searched elsewhere? And *where*
elsewhere?

He had to have a woman. It had been too long, too
goddam long, and he couldn't stand those jutting breasts in
front of him, that hip and leg rubbing against him, for very
much longer. He downed his beer and got rapidly to his
feet. "I've got some unpacking to do," he said. "I'd better
take off."

"I'll see you," said Kilbride.

"Nice to have met you," Blake said to the two girls, and
they said similar things back.

He left the bar and got into the Ford. He felt nervous
and no longer tired, but a little weak. He sat there for a minute, knowing he had to look for a woman, he had to find a
woman. Maybe one of those girls would come out. Maybe,
if he just waited here for a couple of minutes, red-haired

Harriet of the deep breasts would come out and he could offer to give her a ride wherever she was going. He watched the door of the bar, and three college boys came out and packed into the front seat of a convertible. They drove away, hard, the driver hitting the accelerator with too much force.

Where could he look? This wasn't New York or Boston or some other large city, with a red light district or Whore Row. It was just a small town, Winston, twenty two thousand population, supported by an electrical appliance factory, and now it was a college town. A college town, that meant there might be one or two professionals somewhere in the town. But how could he find them? He couldn't ask any of the students. You ask a student where you can find a woman, and the next day the whole student body knows about it and you're finished. You didn't have to be a teacher for a million years to know that. At twenty seven, he could still remember Dan Blake as an undergraduate.

So how the hell could he find a whore? He started the Ford, circled out of the parking lot, drove across the black-topped section of the island that divided the highway, and headed toward town. He stayed to the right lane, the speed-ometer needle quivering on forty, and the other traffic rolled by him. It was almost four in the afternoon, and there weren't many cars headed in toward Winston.

He took the Winston turnoff and drove down the main street of the town. He saw one of the few local cabs, a black Chevy, four years old, with "TAXI" painted in white lettering on the doors, and remembered somebody telling him once that cabbies always knew where the whores could be found. He parked the Ford on a side street and hailed the taxi.

He was embarrassed when he asked the cabdriver, but the driver didn't seem to notice. He said, "This is a small town, Mister."

"I'm not a cop," Blake told him. "I'm a college instructor. This is my first year here. You want to see some identification."

"It might not be a bad idea," said the cabby.

Blake handed over his wallet, and the cabby held it until he was stopped by a red light. He leafed through the plastic windows in the wallet, and Blake handed him the letter from the college, accepting him, which he was still keeping in his inside jacket pocket, he wasn't sure why. The cabby was satisfied, and handed the wallet and letter back to him. "This is a small town," he said again. "Things come pretty high in a small town."

"How much?"

"Probably twenty dollars."

Blake licked his lips. He had twenty-six dollars in his wallet. He knew the cabby had looked at it, counted the money in his wallet, and was fixing the price accordingly. He should have taken the money out first. He said, "That's too much. You saw how much money I had. I don't get paid for two weeks."

"I don't set the price, Mister," said the cabby, though they both knew he was lying. "That's up to the girl. And twenty is just about the cheapest you can get."

He was being held up, and he knew it. He should tell the cabby to stop, he should get out and go back to the Ford and climb in and drive back to the campus and forget the whole thing. He was being held up and he couldn't afford it. He waited, nervous and not tired and just slightly weak, and then he said, "All right."

"I'll make a call," said the cabby.

They drove another two blocks, before the cabby parked near a drugstore. He looked back at Blake. "You got anything on you, Mister?"

"No."

"You need something. For your own protection, as well as the girl's. Give me fifty cents, I'll get you a pack while I'm making the call."

He didn't have fifty cents in change, so he gave the cabby a dollar, then waited, fidgeting, ashamed of himself already, wishing he hadn't started this, until the cabby came back and said, "All set." He handed a small metal box, like an aspirin box, back to Blake, then started the cab's motor.

"Where's my change?" Blake asked him.

The cabby looked disgusted. He fumbled in his pocket and handed Blake forty cents. Blake looked at it. "I paid for the phone call?"

"That's right."

They were silent on the way. The cabby drove around town for a while, as though aimlessly, then stopped at a corner and a girl climbed into the back seat. She was young, as young as the girls in the bar, but she was thinner than they, with older, more faded clothing, and a thin, pale face. Her hair was black and long and straight, and she looked at him without interest. "I'm Annette," she said.

Like hell you are, he thought. "My name's Herman," he told her.

She didn't smile. It would have been all right, he wouldn't have minded any more, if she had only smiled. But she didn't smile. She looked at him seriously and said, "Hello, Herman."

"Hello, Annette," he said, and he hated her.

The cabby drove through town and beyond, along a curving, two lane secondary road that twisted up through scrubby forest land, and finally turned off onto a dirt road. He stopped finally, and killed the engine. "I'll take a walk," he said, and got out of the car.

Blake watched him walk away, down the dirt road and around a curve. He wondered if the cabby would circle back and watch from the trees. Probably.

There was a blanket on the shelf behind the back seat. Annette picked it up and got out of the car. They were both silent. He helped her spread the blanket, then watched her as she methodically undressed. Her face was passive and expressionless, and when she was nude, she lay on her back on the blanket and looked at him. "Aren't you going to get undressed?"

"Yes." He removed his clothing and lay with her.

She was terrible. She lay rigid, unmoving, uncaring, with her face, still expressionless, turned away from him. He knew the cabby was watching, he knew they were both feeling contempt for him, but it didn't matter. His passion caught him up and buried him and he groveled.

When it was over, she put on her shoes and walked into the forest, while he put his clothes back on. She came back a few minutes later, dressed, folded the blanket, put it back on the shelf, and honked the car horn. Her face was still passive, still expressionless.

They sat together in the back seat. After a minute, the cabby came trudging up the road toward them. The girl said, "You can pay me now."

He paid her. On the way back to town, he stared out the window, not wanting to look at either of them. They let him off in the center of town and he walked to the Ford. He climbed in and drove back to the campus.

2

REGISTRATION WAS A MESS. It took place in the school gymnasium, where card tables and folding chairs had been set up in a huge rectangle around the basketball court. The finance and administrative people were at the tables nearest the door, with the instructors at the rest of the tables. A crudely-lettered sign was thumb-tacked to the front edge of each table, dividing the teacher's name and the classes he was to be in charge of.

Registration was to start at nine. Blake arrived at the gymnasium just after nine and found his own table, with BLAKE, DANIEL, ENGLISH 101, SEC. 4, 5, 6, 7, ENGLISH 307, SEC. 1, printed on the card. He sat down in the uncomfortable folding chair, and waited for the influx of students. Each student would be given a class card, in return for his or her tuition money, and would then go to the correct tables to have the card signed by the proper teachers. The teachers, in their turn, would make up the class rosters from the cards. It was, in theory, a smooth operation, but it never seemed to work out that way.

There was no smoking allowed in the gym, but there was an ashtray on Blake's table. He looked around and saw many of the other teachers smoking, and remembered what Kilbride had said about the extra privileges of faculty. Gratefully, he lighted a cigarette. He was still a little shaky. After the useless encounter with the whore, Annette, he had gone back to his apartment, intending to get rid of the evening by reading, and had remembered too late that all of his books were in his office. He started for the office, to get a book, and wound up at Monequois Inn. But the bar was jammed with students, and he found himself looking at the girls in a way that someone might eventually notice. The twenty dollars had been wasted. Annette hadn't satisfied the need, she had only made it stronger, by making the memories more clear in Blake's mind. The undergraduate chatter annoyed him, and the undergraduate girls made him nervous. He finally left and drove to town, where he spent the last of his money on a fifth of good vodka. Returning to his apartment, he broke out the ice cubes, used tap water for a chaser, and sat in the dark living room, brooding and drinking, until he had gone to sleep.

And now he was hung over. And he was stiff, from having slept sitting up. His hands were shaking a bit, and the echoing sounds of conversation and shoes on the wood floor, magnified by the high hollowness of the gymnasium, were giving him a dull headache. He smoked a cigarette, and waited for the students to start coming through.

Monequois College boasted a student body of nearly twelve hundred. Over half of these, six hundred and fifty, were freshmen. The school had been growing each year since its face lifting, but was noted for being rough on grades. A quarter of these freshmen would flunk out the first semester, and another quarter would flunk out at the end of the year. Probably three hundred of them would become sophomores at Monequois, and the weeding would continue, until the senior year, when probably a hundred seniors would graduate. Blake remembered a joke from his own undergraduate days. Reporter: How many students in your school, Professor? Professor: One in a hundred.

And I'll probably never get to see that one, Blake thought. The first of the freshmen were moving uncertainly across the basketball court now, having paid their tuition and been given their class cards. Since freshmen all took the same courses, their class cards had already been filled out for them, and all they had to do was find the proper teachers. Since the freshmen didn't know what any of the teachers looked like, and since the lettering on the name-and-course cards was too small to be seen more than three feet away, congestion had set in by nine-thirty.

Blake watched the freshmen wandering by, peering at the card attached to his table, glancing swiftly at him and swiftly away again, and then moving vaguely on to the next table, to read the next card and peek at the next teacher. He felt sorry for them, the way an observer always feels sorry for the dehumanized sheep of a processing line, but at the same time he found them funny. He watched them, and wondered when one of them would stop at his table and put him to work. One hundred and twenty of these freshmen would be his, for him to teach their native language to, and one of the hundred and twenty should be stopping by pretty soon.

One finally did, and Blake wasted a few seconds staring. This one was nearly six feet, five inches tall. He had a full, glorious red beard, neatly trimmed, that surrounded his entire jawline, and he was dressed in a modest gray suit, blue tie and white shirt. Most of the other freshmen were in slacks, flannel shirts and zipper jackets.

The bearded student said, "Doctor Blake?" His voice was deep, to go with his size and beard, and he stood at ramrod attention, staring at a point just above Blake's head.

"Mister Blake," he corrected, automatically. Then he said, "You're a freshman?"

"Yes, sir."

Then it hit him. "G. I. Bill?"

"Yes, sir."

And you haven't been out very long, either, Blake thought. He snapped, "Name, rank, serial number."

"Matheson, Gregory S., Airman First Class, AF12-451995."

"When'd you get out?"

"Last week, sir. Early out for education."

"Look at my shoulders," said Blake.

Matheson was obviously puzzled, but he did as he was told. Blake watched his eyes move from that imaginary point in mid-air, and look at each of Blake's shoulders in turn. The puzzlement lasted a second or two longer, and then Matheson smiled. "Gets to be a habit, sir," he said.

"No bars on the shoulders," said Blake.

Matheson relaxed, moving out of his rigid attention pose. "I'll get used to things, sir," he said.

"Do you think you'll get used to not saying sir?"

"I think so, sir." Matheson grinned. "In a year or two."

"How old are you?"

"Twenty-six, si—twenty-six."

A year younger than I. And I'm going to teach him—freshman English. "How long were you in?"

"Eight years. I took a second hitch."

Eight years? Blake remembered his own six months of active duty, and how delighted he was when it was over. "Why so long?" he asked.

"I liked Japan." Matheson grinned again. "Then I liked Germany after that."

"We're new here together," Blake told him. He pointed at the white card in Matheson's hand. "What am I supposed to do with that, do you know?"

"Sign it, I think, sir." Matheson handed over the card. "Next to the course I'm taking from you."

Blake studied the card, then shuffled the class rosters he had found on the table when he came in. Matheson was in Section 5. He copied the name from the card to the class roster and signed the card. He gave the card back to Matheson. "See you in class," he said.

"Right, sir." Smiling, Matheson tossed him a salute, and Blake answered it.

The next was a girl, fresh from high school and terrified by confusion. She was the type who talks in whispers, afraid someone will hear her. Blake kept asking her to speak up, but it wasn't any use. She was in Section 7. He went through the paperwork, handed the card back, and she crept on.

They came in a flood after that, high school boys and girls and a smattering of veterans, and there were times when a line extended, ten deep, away from his table. There was no longer time to meet each student, to connect name and face. He scribbled his name, filled out the class rosters, and said, "Next." After a while, he noticed that all the veterans were going into Section 5. He wondered about that, but he didn't have much time for speculation. He handed the card back and said, "Next."

It was supposed to be over at twelve, but it wasn't. The freshmen kept moving through until nearly one o'clock, when the upperclassmen were supposed to start. Blake was just beginning to notice his stomach, when Kilbride came over and said, "How about some lunch?"

"It's ten minutes to one. Isn't there another batch coming at one o'clock?"

"Afternoon registration never starts on time. These are upperclassmen. They know the score. There won't be a one of them here before one-thirty. Come on, let's get something to eat at the faculty snack bar."

They left the gymnasium and walked across a lawn to the Faculty Club. The snack bar was to the right as you went in, with music rooms, ping-pong rooms and the television room off to the left.

The snack bar was crammed. It had a seating capacity almost as large as the number of teachers at the school, and the entire faculty, it seemed, was eating lunch here at the same time. Blake followed Kilbride through the cafeteria line, and they found an empty table in a distant corner. They were barely seated when a girl, holding a full tray, stopped in front of them and said, "Is this seat empty?"

"Surely," said Kilbride. He and Blake both got up, helped the girl put the tray down, helped her move the plates and cups and glasses from the tray to the table, and then sat down again to look at her and introduce themselves.

"Ann Shallcross," she told them. "I'm new here. Girls' Phys Ed instructor."

Blake and Ann Shallcross were both quiet during the meal, as Kilbride talked steadily about the horrors of registration, faculty politics, which members of the faculty were idiots, and how unlikely it was to find a spark of intelligence in a freshman. Blake spent the time studying Ann Shallcross. She looked to be about twenty-five and, in answer to a question of Kilbride's, she said yes, this was her first year teaching, she had gotten her M.A. just in June, so she was possibly even younger than twenty-five. Maybe twenty-three. She had blonde-brown hair, cut short and brushed severely, but becomingly, close to her head, straight back without a part. Her face was square and strong looking, but still feminine. Her eyes were too firm, her lips a bit too thin, for real beauty, but she was still a good looking woman, one of the better looking women Blake had met. Her body was slender and solid. She was dressed in a short-sleeved white blouse and a black skirt, and her breasts were small and out-thrust, her waist narrow, her hips gently curving, looking as though they would be smooth to the touch.

This was the woman. He knew it right away. Not a student, but still close by, accessible. She looked as though she would be good in bed, strong and active, not passive and uncaring like that stupid whore in town.

Blake looked around the room and saw others of the younger faculty members glancing over at Ann Shallcross. There were other women on the teaching staff, but none of them were young or good looking. Blake knew he would be fighting the whole damn faculty, and probably some of the student veterans, too. But he was here first, or at least he hoped he was, and he wanted to establish a beachhead be-fore anybody else could move in.

He didn't have to worry about Kilbride. Kilbride was married and lived in town. He listened to Kilbride talking, and waited impatiently for the man to shut up, so he could start talking to Ann himself.

But Kilbride talked the whole lunchtime away, and then they were on their way back to the gymnasium, Ann walking between them, and Kilbride was still talking. Finally, Blake broke in. He said, "Where did you take your Master's?"

"A little school down in Georgia," she said. "I don't sup-pose you've ever heard of it."

"Try me."

"McClintock College."

"Sure," he said. He smiled with relief. "I knew someone who taught there. Jeff Collinswood. We had the same agent."

A common ground. Blake relaxed as Ann talked about Jeff Collinswood, and gradually he allowed the conversation to move to that word, "agent," and told her, with just the right degree of modesty, that yes, he was the author of *Drink Deep The Night*. Then they were at the gymnasium and she said, "See you later."

"Snack bar?" he asked. "For dinner?"

"Sure. Bye now."

He watched her walk across the gymnasium floor, a tall, athletic girl with good legs supporting a good body, and Kilbride said, "You made a hit there, Dan."

"I hope so," said Blake.

The afternoon moved at a snail's pace. These were upper-classmen who were being registered now, and the only ones who would be coming to see him would be in his Intermediate

Creative Writing course. These came along slowly, and he had time to chat with them, get to know them. By the end of the afternoon, he had eight students in the writing course, five juniors and three seniors. Three of the juniors and one of the seniors were girls, which made a class evenly divided according to sex.

It became obvious to him by the fourth enrollment in the class that the people who were taking this course were all motivated, at least partially, by the fact that he was a published novelist. He got the impression from some of them, particularly the girls, that this was the only motivating factor. None of the eight seemed to him, on a first meeting, to have much strong potential as writers, though one, a junior named Dave Markham, had sold one short story, a few months previously, to a penny-a-word science fiction magazine. Blake asked him whether the story had been published yet or not, and Markham, a short, pale, spectacled boy with skin trouble, told him it was on the stands now. Blake made a mental note to read the story.

By four-thirty, registration was complete. It was too early for dinner, but Blake decided to go to the snack bar anyway, on the possibility that Ann Shallcross would be there. He left the gymnasium, and saw her walking ahead of him, toward the snack bar. He called to her, and she waited for him, smiling as he ran to catch up.

"How did you do this afternoon?" she asked him.

"Got eight enrollments in the writing course. How about you?"

"I really didn't have anything to do. My only classes are with the freshman girls. I helped the people in the business department."

"Listen," said Blake. "That snack bar is going to be a mess again. Let's not go there."

"Where else?"

"I have a car," he said. "Let's drive to town. There must be at least one quiet place in town where we can get a decent meal and something to drink with it."

"I'll have to change," she said.

"It's early yet anyway. I ought to change, too. Shall we do it?"

She smiled. "I'd like to. I haven't been away from the campus for three days, ever since I got here. You don't know how lucky you are to have a car."

"Not this car," he said. "Where do you live? Do you need a ride?"

"No, I'm right across the street, in the faculty building."

"Oh. Oh, of course."

They walked across the campus to the main gate, and over the highway to the faculty building. The faculty building was a long, shallow, two-story-high structure, filled with apartments for the unmarried teachers. Each apartment contained a living room, a bedroom, a kitchen, a bath and a closet, and all were furnished with identical chairs and tables and rugs. The apartments were numbered from left to right, the first floor apartment at the far left being number one, the one above it number two, then three and four next to them, and so on. Blake lived on the second floor, apartment twelve, and he discovered that Ann was his next-door neighbor to the left, in apartment ten. Each apartment had a private entrance, so that there were double sets of doors spaced across the front of the building.

"Last one changed," said Blake, as they reached the building, "is a rotten egg."

"You're on."

He unlocked the downstairs door and hurried up the stairs to his apartment. He had been too shaky to shave this morning, and the stubble was plain on his face by now. He shaved, rapidly, nicking himself twice, and changed clothes. It occurred to him that Ann was just on the other side of the wall, changing *her* clothes, and when he concentrated, he could almost see her, slipping out of her clothing, walking naked across the room to the bureau and the closet—He had to be careful. He couldn't rush this thing, couldn't expect her to come to bed with him the first day he saw her. Today, he would be a perfect gentleman. He would follow her lead, and wait.

She was waiting for him when he got downstairs, so he was the rotten egg. She had changed to a sleeveless light blue dress and white heels, and she looked younger and prettier than ever. They smiled at each other, and he took her arm. They walked around the building to the parking lot and climbed into the Ford.

They were halfway to town before it occurred to him that he didn't have any money. He was petrified for just a second, trying desperately to think of what he could do. He could say he'd forgotten his wallet, drive back to school, borrow some money—from whom? The only one he knew was Kilbride, and he had probably gone home already.

He had unconsciously taken his foot off the accelerator, and the car was slowing, as traffic rushed by him. He became aware of Ann, looking at him with puzzlement, and he decided the only thing he could do was tell her the truth. "I just remembered something," he said. "Something embarrassing. I don't know how to tell you."

"What?"

He pulled the car over to the dirt shoulder of the road and stopped. He looked at her. "I'm broke," he said. "I—I spent all my money getting here, and I forgot all about it when I asked you out. I feel like an idiot." He grinned with embarrassment. "The dollar I spent on lunch today was the last. I've got thirty cents to my name."

"Oh," she said. Then she smiled. "Don't look so worried. It isn't as bad as all that."

"It's just embarrassing," he said.

She opened her purse. "I don't think I have enough—"

"No, no. That makes it even worse. No, I don't want to borrow any money from you."

"Do you have any food at home?" she asked him.

"Some," he said. "Bread and eggs and things."

"So do I. Between your kitchen and mine, we should be able to get a meal together. How does that sound?"

"Fine," he said. "Sure. If you want to—"

"I'm a lousy cook. I feel I ought to warn you."

"Payday," he said, "I buy you filet mignon."

"It's a deal."

He started the car again, and drove until he found a place where he could cross the island and head back in the other direction again. He was grateful to her for having made things so easy for him. It could have been a mess. How could he have forgotten like that? Stupidity. All kinds of stupidity. Stupidity to have spent his money on that whore in the first place, and then meet a girl like Ann the next day, and be broke.

They drove back to the faculty building and left the Ford in the parking lot. As they walked around front, she said, "Let's check your kitchen first. We can go across to my place through the back porch. Won't have to come all the way downstairs."

"Fine," he said, and he was thinking about the future.

She took over in the kitchen. He had saved the brown paper bag from the grocery store, and now he opened it and filled it with the things she chose from the refrigerator and pantry shelves. Then they left his apartment, via the back door. Each apartment had a back porch, and a clothesline extending out to a pole at the edge of the parking lot, and the back porches were connected by doors. They went to her kitchen, an exact replica of his, and he put the sack of groceries on the kitchen table.

"Go on in the living room and sit down," she said, "while I play chef. My record player's in there, and some records. Pick something out."

"Fine," he said. He started for the hallway to the living room and stopped. "Listen," he said. "Thank you."

"Poo. I know what broke is."

He grinned and went into the living room. The record player was a small portable, set up on the coffee table, which had been moved from in front of the sofa and placed against one wall, near the electricity outlet. A stack of long-playing record albums was on the floor beside it. Blake looked through the albums, most of which were the many-violined mood music type, and finally chose one at random. They all looked exactly alike to him, and most of them would sound pretty much alike, too. His own taste was for modern jazz of the west coast variety.

When he opened the top of the portable, he saw it had an automatic changer, so he put a whole stack of records on, pushed the lever, and closed the top again. As the music streamed out, he walked back to the kitchen.

"I just remembered something," he said. "I have some vodka next door. No chaser, though."

"That's all right with me," she said. "I'm a vodka and water girl myself."

"Same here." They smiled at each other. Another common ground. "I'll go get it. Be right back."

He hurried next door. Now, what had he done with the vodka? He was sure he hadn't finished it all. He looked around the kitchen, didn't see it, and continued the search in the living room. He found it at last, half-full, beside the chair where he had slept last night. He brought it back with him and said, "Glasses."

"Top shelf," she said, pointing to the cabinets above the sink. She was mixing something in a bowl.

"Heavy on the vodka or heavy on the water?"

"Half-and-half," she said.

"Coming up." He got two glasses, sloshed vodka and tap water into each, brought an ice cube tray out of the refrigerator and plunked one ice cube into each glass. He handed one drink to Ann, and they toasted each other.

As she continued getting dinner ready, he sat at the kitchen table, nursing his drink, and said, "Tell me about you."

"Tell you what?" She was measuring things, stirring things, and didn't look at him when she talked.

"Who you are, where you're from, what you think, the whole thing."

"The whole thing? In one evening?" She looked at him, then, and smiled.

"Just skim the surface," he said.

"One second." She had made a casserole, and she slid the bowl into the oven, then sipped from her drink and put it back on top of the refrigerator. She grabbed another bowl, started measuring again. "Name," she said, "Ann Shallcross. Race, Caucasian. Height, five-seven. Weight, one hundred thirty—well, thirty-five. Age, twenty-four." She paused. "Let's see, what else do they ask on those employment questionnaires?"

"Sex?"

She grinned at him. "We've barely met." But he knew it was only a joke, not an invitation. "Let's see," she said. "Color of eyes, blue. Color of hair—I say blonde, everybody else says brown. What do you say?"

"Blonde."

"Flatterer. Uh, employment history. I've been a park counselor every summer for the last six years. I was a part-time salesgirl in a department store while I was going to college. That's all. Not a very good employment background, is it?"

"You filled out a lot of these things?"

"Over fifty. Nobody believes a twenty-four-year-old girl can be capable of teaching in college. Not even Phys Ed. The only reason I got this job is because I have an uncle with connections. A very important man in the state capital. An assemblyman, in fact."

"Well, well. I'm in the presence of greatness."

"Now it's your turn," she said. "I know you wrote a book, a very good book, but that's all I know."

"Have you read the book?"

She hesitated. "Truthfully?"

"Truthfully. I wrote it three years ago. It doesn't really matter any more."

"Then I didn't," she said. "But I'd like to," she added. "Very much. I've heard people talk about it, say it was a very good book."

"You don't have to read it," he told her. "Really."

"I want to anyway. I know the author. This way, I'll get to know the author even better. Now, come on, you were going to fill out the form, too."

He did. He told her about himself, the surface facts, leaving out the five books that hadn't sold, the letter from the agent, the letter from the assistant editor, the phone call to the agent, all the unpleasant things of the last few years. He summed up the last three years in two words: "I loafed."

Then they ate. She was a very good cook, and he told her so, and they chatted, casual and friendly together. He realized that they were still on the surface together, still chatting with that aimlessness and lack of depth inevitable when two people have just met, but he couldn't think of any way to change the mood. They *had* just met. They had very little in common, identical apartments, new jobs at the same college, one mutual friend whom neither knew very well, and a shared taste for vodka and water. Not anywhere near enough to build any meaningful relationship on. But they were getting to know each other, just a bit, and with proximity they would start sharing experiences and happenings and meanings. With time, the relationship very well could deepen. Unless the urgency and impatience straining inside him burst out and spoiled the whole thing.

After dinner, they moved to the living room. The records were still playing, soft violin music that was neither offensive nor memorable, and he suggested that they dance. She was a very good dancer, much better than he, and the feeling of her waist against his arm, her breasts touching his chest, agitated the impatience and the urgency again, and he fought himself for control. They danced close together, their legs brushing, her one hand at the back of his neck, her hair soft against his cheek, and he was too afraid of making a mistake, of rushing things, to be able to think of anything to say. She was silent, too, but it never occurred to him that she might be silent for the same reason. It grew dark, with one lamp lit in the living room, and he turned the stack of records over. Music whispered into the room again, and when he crossed to her, to dance again, she was smiling at him and her eyes were bright. She extended her arms out toward him, and he stood close to her, staring into her eyes and feeling his heart pounding in terror and hope.

Her hand rested against the back of his neck again, the contact like an electric shock, and he put his hands on her waist, drawing her against him. Her lips were parted slightly, fuller than they had seemed this afternoon, full and moist, and she made a tiny sound in her throat when he kissed her. His hands were clamped at her waist, pulling her against him, and he stared at her face as they kissed. Her eyes were closed, and her lips were warm, demanding.

Without speaking, they moved to the sofa. They sat side by side and he kissed her again, his arms tight around her, her head back against the top of the sofa back. His right arm was imprisoned between her body and the sofa, but his left arm was free, and he touched his fingers to her cheek, caressing her cheek and throat and arm. His hand slid from her arm to her side, stroking her side, feeling the bra strap beneath the dress. He moved his head forward, kissing her cheek and her neck and her ear, gently nipping her earlobe between his teeth, and she made a soft, trembling sound, half moan and half sigh. He stroked her side and his fingers spread, just touching the first roundness of her breast, and she trembled beneath his hand. He kissed her throat, the line of her jaw, kissed her lips again, his tongue reaching out to touch her lips, and her lips parted for him. He stroked her side, brushed his hand across the flatness of her stomach, curved around her side again, and up, to the first rise of her breast. He moved his hand against her breast, feeling the nipple firm and out-thrust beneath the clothing, and he squeezed the nipple between his fingers. She groaned, moving suddenly and twistingly beneath him, and his hands fumbled eagerly for the buttons of her dress. There were buttons extending down the front of the dress, between her breasts, down as far as her waist. With clumsy haste, he opened the front of her dress, and they separated long enough for him to the clothing, and he squeezed the nipple between his slip down her arms and free. Her eyes stayed closed, and she drew him close to her again, kissing him, her hands moving on his back.

Her breasts were not large, but they were firm and strong, curving outward even without the bra. He kissed her breasts, biting the nipples, and his left hand reached down to her knee, stroked the inside of her legs, pushing the skirt up to her hips. Their breathing was loud in the room, and their hands roamed each other's bodies, hot and damp and clutching.

But when he tried to push her down on the sofa, her eyes opened and she whispered, "No. Please, Dan, no. Don't."

The force was too strong in him to let him speak. He leaned against her, his hands rapid on her body, pushing her backward. She struggled against him now, her eyes open and fearful. "No. We can't. Dan, don't, we can't."

She pulled away from him, getting to her feet, and backed across the room, pulling her slip and the top half of her dress back into place. He started after her and she stood trembling as he put his arms around her. "Ann," he whispered. "Ann, come to bed with me."

"I can't," she whispered. "Oh, please. I'm sorry. It's my fault, I shouldn't have let it start, please, no, I can't." She freed herself from his arms and they stood staring at each other, both shaken and weak. "Dan, I'm sorry," she said. "I'm so sorry, I really am, I know what I'm doing to you, but I can't, I just can't. I didn't know anything like this was going to happen."

"Ann—"

"Please. Don't ask me any more. Don't touch me any more. Please, Dan. I—I'll make us some coffee. I'll be right back, I'll make us some coffee."

She half ran from the living room, and he stood staring after her. He was breathing hard, and he cursed himself, knowing how close he had come, wondering what he'd done wrong, what mistake he had made. Had he gone too fast, been too eager? He stood in the living room, not listening to the music from the record player, and cursed himself for being a fool.

She brought the coffee in after a few minutes. She looked at him and smiled, hesitantly, apologetically. "Some coffee," she said.

"Thank you." He took the cup from her and looked at her, wondering what he'd done wrong.

"I'm sorry," she said again. "I really am. I didn't mean for anything like that to happen. Are you disgusted with me?"

"No," he said automatically. Then, truthfully, "No. I was wondering if you were disgusted with me."

She shook her head. "It was my fault, I let it happen. Sit down, come on, let's sit down." She sat on the sofa. Her bra was still there, and she pushed it behind her, out of sight. Her dress was buttoned now, and he could see the outline of her breasts, the nipples still hard. "Sit down," she said again.

"On the sofa?"

"You're mad at me."

"No." He sat beside her on the sofa. "No, I'm not. I'm mad at myself."

"For what?"

"For failing."

She looked away from him, stared at her coffee cup. "It would have been a mistake," she said. "We were both lonely, that's all, in a new place, not knowing anybody, both a little depressed. It wouldn't have been any good."

"You'd be good," he told her.

"Don't talk like that. I'm still a little—excited." She looked at him, a young and serious girl, wanting him to understand. "Don't you see that it wouldn't have been any good? Tomorrow, and the day after tomorrow—"

"You'd still be good."

"We'd be embarrassed with each other. You'd think I was just a tramp, I'd sleep with anybody as soon as I met him, and I'd know you were thinking it. We'd avoid each other, and dislike each other, and that would spoil the whole thing."

"All I know is that I want you," he said. She was still excited, as she'd said. Maybe it would still work out. Maybe talk would succeed, where touch had failed. "I don't think you're a tramp," he said. He put his hand on her knee as he talked. "I think you're a lovely girl, a desirable girl, and I want to go to bed with you. And then I want to eat breakfast with you, and lunch and dinner, and go to bed with you again, and just keep repeating it, over and over again."

She put the coffee cup on the drum table beside the sofa, and got to her feet. "Don't talk about it any more," she said. "Dan, this isn't just an excuse, but I've got a headache. I really do. It's probably nerves or something. I think we ought to say goodnight."

So it was lost. For tonight, anyway. He set his coffee cup down and stood beside her. "All right," he said. "I'm sorry. I—got too eager, I got carried away. We won't talk about it any more."

"I like you very much," she said. "I'm glad you came to this school."

"So am I. Would it be all right if I kissed you good night?"

She smiled. "I think so. But just a little kiss."

"All right." He kissed her, and felt the urgency rising through him again. His arms tightened around her, and she shook her head, backing away. "I'm sorry," he said. "Maybe we should just shake hands."

She laughed. "Even that might be too much. Maybe we ought to just wave to each other."

"Good idea." He waved at her, smiling, and she waved back. They walked through the apartment to the back door, where he stopped and said, "Listen, shall we eat breakfast together anyway?"

"We might as well," she said. "I have all your food. When's your first class?"

"Nine."

"Me, too. I'll see you at eight-thirty."

"If not," he said, "it means I didn't hear the alarm, so hammer on the wall or something."

"I will."

He walked back to his own apartment, and through to the living room, turning lights on as he went. He suddenly remembered the vodka, still in Ann's kitchen. He decided not to go back after it. He was at a delicate state in the relationship between him and Ann. If he was patient—God, if he could only be patient for once in his life!—if he was patient, they would have a good time together. But if he worked too hard, got too eager, she'd put him down as an oversexed wolf, and that would be the end of that. Going back again now, no matter how legitimate the excuse, would be a mistake.

He wandered around the living room, thinking about Ann, thinking about her body beneath his hands, and he wondered what he could do for the rest of the evening. It was barely nine o'clock, far too early to go to bed, and he was too nervous to sleep anyway. His books were still over in the damn office, he had no radio, no record player and no television set, and he didn't have the money to go out anywhere.

He prowled the apartment, restless and uneasy, and noticed his portable typewriter, in its case on the floor in the bedroom. He took it out and set it on the writing desk next to his bed. There was paper already in one of the desk drawers, and he slipped a sheet into the machine and stared at it. He could write something, to get rid of the time. Write what? He stared at the typewriter and the blank sheet of paper, and after a while he decided to write himself a letter. He would write himself a letter, telling himself what was going on with himself.

He started: "Dear Dan," and wrote, at first, about the college, and the classes he was to teach, and the students he had met. Then he wrote about Ann, describing her, describing the things they had done together this evening, describing the things he still wanted to do with her, using whatever language came first into his head. He wrote about the girl students, and what he thought when he looked at them, and then he came to the end of a paragraph, double-spaced, and wrote, "If I had twenty dollars now, I would go see Annette." He pulled the paper from the machine, threw it into the wastebasket, and stared at the wall.

3

REGISTRATION HAD BEEN ON TUESDAY and classes started the next day. Blake had all four of the Freshman English classes on Wednesday, at nine, ten, one and three. The first meeting of his Intermediate Creative Writing class wasn't till Thursday at two.

He got up on time Wednesday morning, fidgety and irritable, wishing he'd found some other sort of job. He didn't want to play at being a teacher, and he knew that was all he could do, play at it.

His mood improved when he went next door to see Ann. She looked young and bright, with a flower-patterned apron over her blue skirt and white blouse, and breakfast was ready for him when he arrived. They talked about school while they ate, both of them avoiding any mention of the night before, and then left together, to walk across the highway to the campus. They parted at the gymnasium, and Blake strolled down one of the meandering side roads, lined with classroom buildings, to building five, room 512. Classes

started at ten after the hour, ending on the hour, and he was
a good ten minutes early. So was half the class. He sat at his
desk, at the front of the room, feeling alone and unsure of
himself, while the freshmen chattered in front of him.
Gradually, the class filled, and the sound of the chattering
increased. There was a clock on the back wall, behind the
students, and Blake watched it, waiting for the class to start.
He waited until twelve after, but the chattering kept on, and
he realized he was going to have to start the class himself,
without any assistance from the students. Somehow, he had
to attract their attention, and he wasn't sure how. He was
nervous, and he knew he was feeling stage fright. As soon as
he opened the class, thirty people would all be looking at him
at once.

He took a deep breath, held it, and got to his feet. One
or two of the students glanced at him, but the rest continued
their conversations. He cleared his throat. Nothing happened. Loudly, he said, "Class."

The conversations stopped, at once. In the silence, they
looked at him. This was their first day, too, and he realized
they were as unsure as he was. He said, "My name's Blake.
Mister, not Doctor. I'll call the roll now. If you don't hear
your name, let me know."

He went through the role slowly, trying to couple each
name with each face. It was impossible, but he tried anyway.
Then he outlined for them what the class would be doing
that semester. Freshman English was mainly a reading
course. They read classics and wrote themes about them.
Themes would be due once every two weeks. Their first reading assignment was Homer's *Iliad*, and they were to read to
page sixty-four for the next class, which would be tomorrow.

Were there any questions? There weren't. Nor was there anything else for him to do, so he dismissed the class. It was nine-thirty.

His next class was in the same room, so he stayed there and read some of the *Iliad* himself. It had been years since he'd opened the book, and he really should know something about it. They would have class discussions, and he should give the appearance that he knew a little something about the course he was teaching.

The ten o'clock class was full of veterans. There wasn't a non-veteran in the class, and the faces that turned to look at him when he called order this time were neither as young nor as doubtful as they had been at nine. They were more serious, more respectful, and more knowing. This would be the most interesting freshman class, but the most dangerous. They would know when he was bluffing, or bored, or unsure.

He called the roll, and the answers were crisp from the ones most recently discharged, overly sloppy from those who had been civilians for a while. Once again, he explained the course, gave the assignment, and dismissed the class. When they got to their feet, the red-bearded Matheson towered above them all. He grinned at Blake, and Blake grinned back. Matheson had been the first student he had met, and he felt a kinship with him. They were both brand new, both trying out a new and strange world. The class lined out of the room, Matheson talking with two or three others, and Blake thought, that's the difference between us. He isn't alone in the new world, I am.

He was free now, until one. And he needed some money. He went to the business office to see about getting an advance "on his pay. The manager, a short, stuffy, numerical type with thinning hair, was a little upset about it at first, since pay advances were not supposed to be given, but Blake pointed out that he was broke and would die of starvation before payday, which might reflect on the school. He got his money.

He had lunch alone in the faculty snack bar and went to his office to wait for his one o'clock class. He read the *Iliad* for a while, but found it boring. He swiveled around in his chair, to look out the window, but the window was too high to see anything through it except the overhang of the roof. He smoked a cigarette, and tried to get interested in the *Iliad*.

Kilbride passed by after a while, and stopped in the doorway to say, "Well, how's it going?"

"All right, I suppose. I took roll, gave the assignments and dismissed the class. I did it twice so far, and it worked both times."

Kilbride laughed. "You keep wondering when they'll catch on, when they'll realize you aren't really a teacher."

"Exactly. By the way, I have one class full of ex-G.I.'s. Are they being segregated, or what?"

"They're being segregated. It's something new this year, and only for the freshmen. Veterans are a bad influence on high school graduates. The vets don't seem to do any work, but they make out all right in their courses, and the kids try the same thing. It doesn't work for them."

"It feels strange," said Blake. "All those guys, thirty of them, practically as old as I am, sitting out there looking at me."

"You'll get used to it. Have you eaten yet?"

"A while ago. I have a one o'clock class. I'll have a cup of coffee with you, though."

"Fine."

As they walked across the campus toward the Faculty snack bar, Blake said, "Your first year, did you have doubts? You know, you wonder if maybe you made a mistake, you should have found some other job instead."

"I still have doubts like that," Kilbride told him. He smiled. "Wait till we get into the swing of things. The themes are piling up, waiting to be read, three students in each class are over-cutting and getting good marks anyway, your office is crowded with kids wanting to know why you gave them such low marks, and you haven't had time to read the assigned material yourself. Then you don't have any doubts. You don't have any time to be doubtful."

"It sounds charming," said Blake.

The snack bar was crowded, but Ann wasn't there. Blake dawdled over a cup of coffee, listening to Kilbride, who never seemed to stop talking, and then it was time for his one o'clock class.

He was finished for the day at three-thirty. He stopped off at the office, grabbed three books at random, in order to have something to read at home, and went back to his apartment. He dropped the books on the bed and went out the back door. He knocked on the kitchen door of Ann's apartment, but there was no answer, so he went back to his own place and read some more of the *Iliad*.

She knocked at his door a little after five. She was dressed in pink pedal pushers and a white man's shirt, the shirt tails tied into a knot at her waist. She smiled. "I was wondering if the pauper wanted some dinner," she said.

"The pauper," he told her, "has some money. How about that filet mignon?"

"Really? Do you have enough?"

"I'm loaded. It's glad-rags time."

"I'll be ready in ten minutes," she promised, and hurried away.

He felt good. He'd managed to get through the first day with no calamities, he had some money in his wallet, and Ann had come looking for him. He smiled at his reflection in the mirror as he shaved for the second time that day, and then it occurred to him that he didn't know where the good restaurants were in Winston, or even if there were any. Ann was new here, too, so she wouldn't know either.

Kilbride would know. He went to the living room and looked up the number of Kilbride's home phone in the small, thin Winston phone book. He dialed, waited, and a woman's voice answered. "Is Roger there?" he asked, and she said, "Just a minute, please."

Kilbride came on and Blake asked him to name a good restaurant. Kilbride named the Blue Room on College Road, at the other end of town. It was named College Road because the old campus had been there, prefabricated buildings and Quonset huts, looking more like an expeditionary camp at the South Pole than a college campus. The Blue Room was just beyond the old campus, on the right. He couldn't miss it. Blake thanked him, and returned to his dressing.

The Blue Room was impossible to miss. It was two miles out from town, with billboards scattered along the right of way, telling the distance still to be covered. They passed the old campus, a huddle of squat, faded buildings, and Blake pointed. "A couple of years ago, we would have been teaching there."

"A depressing looking place," she said.

He slowed the Ford, to get a better look at the campus. "I imagine it had personality," he said, "when it was being used, with students and cars and a fresh coat of paint. I imagine people felt as though they were accomplishing something here."

"It certainly didn't have the facilities the new campus has," she said. She was staring critically at the worn, small buildings. "No gym, no theater, no proper labs, no dormitories. I couldn't have liked it there."

"I would have. Much more than at the new campus. It's the difference between the spirit of a guerilla band and the organization of an army. I'm a guerilla type, myself."

She laughed. "I must be an army type, then. I like the creature comforts."

Then a row of trees hid the campus, and a huge blue neon sign proclaimed the Blue Room. It was early, for diners-out, and the dining room, overdone in blue, was nearly empty. A small stage at one end of the dining room was dark and empty, the piano looking as though it had been abandoned years ago. There was entertainment only on weekends.

The steak was delicious and cheap, or it seemed cheap to Blake, who had been used to resort prices for the last few years. As they ate, the room filled, and they were surrounded by the muffled conversation of the other diners. The Blue Room went in for atmosphere in a big way, with blue table-cloths, blue drapes on the walls, and the candles on each table the only source of light. The waitresses were dressed in blue and were almost invisible in the dimness of the room. It was quiet and unhurried and relaxing. After dinner, they drank white wine and smiled at each other over the weaving candle. The waitress took the dirty plates away, and they drank more wine, saying very little to each other, looking at each other and smiling.

It was finally time to leave. Blake paid the check and left too large a tip, and they walked outside to a world that had become night while they were away. It was a clear night, the sky a deep black, powdered with stars. The moon was a week from full, a thick crescent, bright against the sky.

They drove by the old campus again, and Blake looked over at it. The buildings were darker and lower and cleaner in the moonlight, with sharp blocks of light and shadow. Blake said, "Let's look at it."

"All right."

He turned off the road and up the bumpy two-lane entrance to the old campus, parking near the nest of buildings. They got out of the car and walked slowly across the weed-filled, unkempt lawn, listening to the silence and the soft whisper of their passage. The windows were X's against a black background, surrounded by peeling clapboard. Blake leaned close to one of the windows, trying to peer inside, but he couldn't see a thing.

Ann said, "You'd like teaching here, wouldn't you?"

"Yes, I would."

"You're a romantic," she said.

"I know." He looked at her, surprised. "What's wrong with that?"

"Romantics are always getting hurt," she told him.

"Not always. Let's go over this way." He took her hand and they walked deeper among the buildings. Blake pointed.

"The library." It was a Quonset hut, corrugated iron gleaming palely in the moonlight, a weather-beaten LIBRARY sign hanging above the front door. There was a window in the door, and Blake tried once again to look inside, but still couldn't. "The lock's broken," he said. The padlock had been ripped free of the door and was lying on the cement step. "Somebody else was here. Come on, let's go inside."

"There's nothing in there," she said. "Just field mice. Come on, Dan, let's not stay here any longer."

"I just want to see what it looks like inside," he said. He pushed the door open. It was warped and resisted him, creakingly. He stepped through into the darkness. He could see now, just a little bit. Moonlight came through the windows on one side, shining on the litter. Most of the shelves had been removed, and the floor was a mass of rubbish, papers and bits of wood and nails, bent and rusted. Ann followed slowly, hesitantly, as Blake shuffled through the rubbish, peering at the dim shapes. Half a bookcase was left in the middle of the long main room, a mound four feet high, and this was what Blake was moving toward. On the way, he talked to Ann, speaking in a harsh whisper. "The desk was there," he said. "See the marks on the floor? They had paintings on the walls, you can see the squares without dust. The fiction would have been at the back, way at the back, it always is in college libraries."

He had reached the ruin of a bookcase now. It slanted forward, the top remaining shelf splintered and broken. Blake tapped on it, a hollow sound, and a man suddenly stood up from the other side. Blake stepped back involuntarily, bumping into Ann, who gave a quick intake of breath, as though she would scream. The man facing them was tall and heavy and bearded, like paintings of whaler captains, and he was dressed in a frayed and filthy discarded suitcoat over a dark flannel shirt. "Who comes knocking at my door?" he demanded. His voice was deep and slurred, and a strong odor of cheap wine crossed the space between them. "Rap-rap-rapping at my door," he said. "Quoth the Raven, never-more."

Blake stared at him. "Who are you?"

"The ghost of Christmas past." The man chuckled drunkenly and leaned forward against the bookcase. The bookcase lost its balance finally and toppled over, bringing the drunk with it. They crashed to the floor at Blake's feet, and Blake saw another man, a short, thin one like a weasel, who had been sitting on the other side of the bookcase, clutching a gallon jug of wine. The big man, lying on the crumpled bookcase, snorted and laughed, then rolled over onto his back and began to sing. "Roll me o-o-ver, in the clo-o-ver—"

The little one whacked at the singer's ankles. "Hush it, Sammy, there's a lady present!"

The big man sat up at once, the bookcase making a grinding noise beneath him, and said, "A lady present? A lady present? For who? Who is this lady a present for?"

The little one looked up at Blake, blinking and contrite. "We ain't disturbing nothing, Mister. We just come in out of the air, that's all. We'll go quietly. Won't we, Sammy?"

"Who makes Sammy's run?" demanded Sammy.

"Don't mind Sammy," said the little one. "He's a bit drunk."

"We're not police," Blake told him. "You can stay here as long as you want."

"You're a prince!" shouted Sammy, and he had suddenly developed an Irish brogue. "Ye're a prince among min, y'are. Begorrah!" With a rattling of the broken bookcase, he squirmed around and got to his knees. He stared up at Blake. "You're—" he said, then stopped. "No, the light's not good enough. Strike a match like a good boy, Nat, and hold it to the gentleman's face. Don't burn him, now."

Ann was tugging at Blake's arm, whispering, "Come on away, Dan, they're drunk, come on away," but he ignored her. He stood watching the two of them, scrabbling around on the floor, and he smiled, loving them and laughing at them at the same time. Nat weaved to his feet and somehow managed to strike a match. In the glare, Nat's face was pinched and lined, tiny eyes and cheeks and mouth surrounding a long, thin nose. Sammy, still kneeling on the floor, had a massive face, thick eyebrows and beard, a round, bulbous nose, and a high forehead topped by matted, thick black hair. Sammy was squinting at him, pursing his lips, and finally Nat said, "Sammy, the match is burning me fingers."

"Then put it out, you bloody fool," Sammy told him. "He's not the man I thought he was."

"Who did you think I was?" Blake asked him.

The match went out and the room seemed darker than ever. Blake couldn't see Sammy's face any more, when he said, "A writer man, named Blake. Daniel Blake."

Ann was about to say something, but Blake stopped her, squeezing her arm. "Do you know this writer, Blake?"

"Never met the man," said Sammy. "Only through his picture on the dust jacket of his book."

"Sammy's a great reader," said Nat, as though he was proud of being associated with a great reader. "He's read anything you care to name."

"I study the photographs of authors," said Sammy. Boards rattled as he settled himself more comfortably on the floor. "When I read a book," said Sammy, "I like to know a bit about the author thereof. So I study the pictures. You can tell a lot about a man from his picture."

"What about this Blake, the man you thought I was? What did you tell from his picture?"

"A good man," said Sammy, "but a bit too pleased with himself. A writer ought to be thinking about tomorrow's work, not yesterday's. And the book wasn't all that good, anyway. It was a young man's book, and young men don't write great books, no matter what they tell you in the advertisements. I'd like to meet that Blake, I'd like to have a good long chat with him about one thing or another, over a full bottle of vino. Nathaniel, where's the vino? Some vino for our guests."

"I don't think so," said Blake. "We can't stay."

"Stay anyway. We'll have a talk. The books are all gone from here now, there's nothing left to do but talk. Nat, damn you, where's the vino?"

"Right here, Sammy, for God's sake, I've been holding it out to you half an hour or more."

The wine sloshed in the jug as Sammy got his hands on it, and then, with a great clatter of boards and rubbish, he got to his feet and stood swaying in front of them. "A drink," he said. "Join us in a drink. As a host, I'll be greatly disappointed if you don't take a little drink. Nathaniel, do we have a glass for the lady?"

"You know we don't," said Nathaniel. Blake could tell from his voice that he was pouting. "When in the world have we had a glass?"

"We had a mug once. Whatever became of it?"

"You broke it, in a tantrum."

"I never did. No matter. Vino, vino everywhere, and not a glass to scoop with. What's the lady doing all the whispering about?"

"She wants to leave," said Blake.

Sammy nodded, ponderously. "That's the way with women all the time," he said. "She wants to hurry home and touch her frigidaire, to see nobody's stolen it. And what of yourself? Do you want to leave, too?"

"It's late," Blake told him. "We have to leave. I'm sorry."

"No matter. We haven't all that much vino anyways."

"Sammy," said Nat, "you're being surly."

"It doesn't matter a bit," said Sammy. "He isn't the right man, anyways."

"Sammy," said Nat, "that's unkind."

"What in the world," demanded Sammy, "would a world-famous author be doing in a ruint and empty library in a ruint and empty college in a ruint and empty town like Winston anyways? Does it make a bit of sense, Nat?"

"These two is here," said Nat.

"Quirk of fate," said Sammy, "Besides, they're leaving."

"Right now," said Ann. "It was a pleasure to meet you. Come on, Dan."

"Ships passing in the night," said Sammy. "Ships floating in vino."

"Where's the wine, Sammy?" asked Nat.

Blake followed reluctantly after Ann, and behind him the two drunks stumbled and rattled. "Damn me!" roared Sammy. "The backrest is all busted."

"Where's the wine, Sammy? Come on, quit hogging the wine."

They were outside, and Blake pulled the door shut. The moonlight was bright and cold, and a thin breeze ribboned among the buildings, cold between the shoulder blades. The bulky mounds of the buildings hugged the ground, and the breeze rattled loose boards. It was quiet inside the library.

"Your guerillas," said Ann. "Brave mountaineers. Come on, let's go home."

"All right," said Blake. He was wearing a summer suit, and he shivered as they walked back to the car. He wondered if they were cold in the library. Probably not. They had their vino to keep them warm.

Blake got behind the wheel and started the engine. The Ford seemed loud and rickety in the silence surrounding them. He backed the car around, to aim it back at the road again, and someone shouted, "Blake! Hi, Blake! Hey, Blake! Ho, Blake!"

Blake looked at the rear-view mirror and saw Sammy lumbering toward him among the buildings, running with a rolling gait like a bear, Nat scampering behind him. "Hey ho, Blake!" shouted Sammy. "The lady called you Dan! You're the right man after all!"

Ann was prodding his arm. "Hurry, Dan, drive out of here, they're after us. Hurry, they're almost here."

"Hey, *Blake!*"

Blake slammed his foot on the accelerator, and the Ford jounced down the rutted lane to the road. In the mirror, he could see Sammy the bear, standing in front of the building and waving his arms above his head, while Nat the mouse sat on the ground and up-tilted the gallon jug of wine. Then they were at the road and Blake spun the wheel toward town.

They drove for a while in silence, and then Ann said, "Why didn't you want them to know who you were?"

"I wanted to see what they thought about Dan Blake," he said. "And why they were so anxious to meet him. Why did you want to leave?"

"I'm not sure. They frightened me. They were drunk and—I don't know, really. I was just—uncomfortable there."

"I should have stayed," he said. "I should have stayed and talked to them. You could have waited in the car."

"Do you want to go back?"

"No."

"We'll go back, if you want."

"No, I really don't want to. Not any more." He reached out and found her hand. "It's all right, Ann. Don't worry about it."

"I'm sorry," she said. "I was just nervous."

"It's all right, it really is. Listen, you've still got my vodka. How about a nightcap when we get back?"

"All right," she said. He put his arm around her as he drove, and she came close against him, her head resting on his shoulder. "I am sorry, Dan," she said.

"Stop worrying about it. It was just a couple of drunks."

"You wanted to talk to them, though."

"It wouldn't have been interesting, probably. Come on, be quiet for a while."

"All right."

They drove back to the new campus and parked behind the faculty apartment building. They went up the back stairs and through the kitchen door to Ann's apartment. "Go on in and start the records," she said. "I'll make the drinks."

"Okay."

He played the same records, and they sat on the sofa, sipping at their drinks and listening to the music. He put his arm around her, but she said, "We'd better not, Dan. We don't want anything to happen like last night."

"Yes, I do," he said. "I want exactly the same thing to happen. With a different ending."

"Let's just talk," she said.

He put his drink down and took hers out of her hand. "Let's not say a word," he said. He kissed her, and she stiffened, not pulling away, but not responding either. "What's wrong, Ann?" Her eyes were open and she was staring at him as though she were afraid of him. "Ann, what's wrong? Is it me? Don't you like me? Is there something wrong with me?"

She shook her head, but her expression didn't change. "It isn't you," she said.

"Then what is it?"

"I'm afraid," she said. "I'm afraid to."

"I won't hurt you," he whispered. "I'll be careful, I won't hurt you."

"Don't talk like that!" She got to her feet and crossed the room to sit in an armchair. "Let's—let's just have a conversation," she said. "Just talk, that's all."

"Why? Why are you afraid?"

"I just am. Tell me about your classes today. Come on, we'll talk about something else."

"The hell with my classes!" He stood up and glowered at her. "I want to talk about us. You're afraid. Why? Why were you afraid at the old campus? Why are you afraid now? Why are you always so goddam afraid?"

Her face contorted, and she started to cry. "Dan, I'm sorry—"

"Now you're sorry again. The hell with you, the goddam it all to hell with you." He stalked out of the living room, headed toward the back door. On the way through the kitchen, he grabbed his almost-empty vodka bottle, and slammed the porch door behind him. He stormed into his own place, flicking on every light he could find, and threw himself into a chair in the living room to brood. He didn't know why he was so mad at Ann, and he didn't try to ana-lyze it. The evening had started fine, but had soured from the moment they stopped at the old campus. She was stuffy, that's what it was, staid and stuffy, afraid of anything new, anything different or unusual or unconventional. What was it Sammy had said? "She wants to go home and touch her fri-gidaire, to see nobody's stolen it." He had her down pat, he defined her perfectly. Why didn't she go to some suburb and play housewife, and get the hell out of his life? Who needed her, anyway?

He did. No, the hell he did. He needed *a* woman all right, there was no argument there, but not *that* woman, not Ann Shallcross at all. He needed someone who would say, when Sammy asked Nat for a glass for the lady, "I don't need a glass, thanks, just pass the bottle." A woman who got into the goddam *swing* of things, who wasn't afraid of her own blasted shadow. That's why he was mad at Ann Shallcross, though he didn't realize it. He was mad at her because she wasn't the woman he wanted her to be.

There was very little vodka left in the bottle, enough for two or three small drinks, that was all. He'd wasted his damn liquor on the woman, too. Well, three drinks were three drinks, and they'd have to do. He tramped back out to the kitchen and banged things around, making himself a drink.

He was about to go back to the living room when a slight, hesitant tapping sounded at the back door. Now, who the hell? He put the full glass down and hurled open the door.

She was standing there, looking forlorn. "Dan," she said. "Don't be mad at me."

He stared at her. Now she wanted to be his goddam sister or something, he could see it coming from a mile away. "I'm not mad at you," he told her. "I just want to be alone for a while."

"Dan," she said, "I—I won't be afraid any more. Honest."

"What?"

"Can I come in? Just for a little while, and you tell me to leave when you want and I'll go. All right?"

"Listen," he said. He was suddenly ashamed of himself, and didn't want her to carry on like this, as though it had been her fault. "Listen," he said again. "Ann, I'm sorry. I didn't have any right to get sore like that."

"I understand why you did," she told him. "I really do. And you were right." She smiled all at once, the quick, shy smile of a person who hopes you'll smile back. "You left practically a whole drink at my place," she said. "Do you want to come back? We can't waste liquor that way."

"I—sure, all right. And we'll talk about anything you want to. I don't know what got into me, I just got mad at the whole world for a minute, that's all."

"Come on," she said.

He followed her back to her apartment, and they sat down again on the sofa. The two vodka glasses were beside him, and he picked them up, offering one to Ann. "Here," he said. "We'll propose a toast to good manners or something."

"I don't want a drink right now," she said. She was looking at him, and her eyes gleamed in the light from the lamp across the room.

"Neither do I," he said. He put the drinks down and reached for her, and she moved into his arms. When he kissed her, her eyes stayed open, round and bright, staring at him, and she held his hand against her breast. He felt the nipple harden beneath his palm, and he pressed against her, probing her mouth with his tongue. She slid back on the sofa and he lay with her, their lips tight together, their clothing rustling as they moved against one another.

He kissed her throat and her ear, and whispered, "Come to bed, Ann, come to bed."

"Yes. I will."

They got up clumsily from the sofa, and she took his hand, to lead him to the bedroom. Her face was drawn and tense with passion as she stared at him. He undressed her, moving slowly, his hands caressing her, and she raised her head, staring at the ceiling, her body writhing beneath his hands. Her body was slender, but strong and solid, well-tanned, with jutting breasts and flat stomach and warm thighs. They left their clothing in a pile on the floor behind them, and moved silently to the bed. She lay back, her arms reaching up for him, pale and slender in the light, and he moved into her arms.

"Be gentle, Dan," she whispered. "Don't hurt me."

"I won't hurt you. I promise I won't hurt you."

She went rigid suddenly. "Dan!"

"All right. I'll go slow. I won't hurt you, I'll go slow."

"Oh, God. Oh, be careful, Dan, please. Please be careful. There. *There*"

"I'll go slow, I won't hurt you, I'll go slow."

"Go *fast*. Go *fast*."

She clamped him tight to her, and she was all that Annette could have ever been. She twisted and moaned, fighting him, and he clung to her, beating her down, holding her down, until she tensed, her mouth open in a silent scream, and they dissolved, flowed into one.

Then she cried. He lay beside her, out of breath, and she kissed his face and neck and chest, weeping and pressing against him, saying, "Oh, Dan, oh, I'm glad, I'm so glad, I'm glad, oh, darling, I'm so glad."

He held her close to him. "Ann," he whispered. "Ann."

After a while, they slept.

PART TWO
JANICE

4

JANICE WINTHROP WAS ONLY EIGHTEEN YEARS OLD, but she was a college junior. She had skipped the fourth grade, back in grammar school, and had finished high school in three years, including summer sessions. Her first two years of college finished with an A-minus average, numerically 92.2, and she would probably graduate a half year ahead of the class she had entered college with.

In grammar school, Janice Winthrop had perfectly suited the myth that brilliant girls are always ugly. Her body was scrawny and knobby, bony elbows and knees jutting out everywhere, and her head was far too large, teetering atop a thin beanstalk neck. Her eyes were abnormally large, her nose too thin and too long, her mouth too wide, her hair a perpetual mouse-brown mess.

In the last years of high school, however, a transformation had taken place. The body had filled out, with firm, young, well-proportioned breasts, narrow waist, rounded hips and full-fleshed thighs. Her lips had grown more full, her cheekbones more prominent, her eyes deep and dark brown and brooding, her hair a rich chestnut, well-combed. She had suddenly emerged to a gypsy-like beauty, and she was still brilliant.

She gradually became aware of her body. The boys who lately flocked around her made her realize she was no longer the plain, uninteresting girl she had been, with no pleasures other than reading or movie-going with the girls. And her body itself was beginning to make demands. There were other pleasures, now within her grasp, now desired, now available.

But the high school boys and, later, the college boys, held no interest for her. Their lust was too obvious, too impersonal, and too amateurish. None of them ever managed to give her either the impression that *she* individually was desired, nor that they would be very proficient if she did submit. And her father's contemporaries, paunchy, hair-thinning, placid, blind, they were equally useless. Somewhere between adolescence and obsolescence, there had to be men who could satisfy both her body and her mind.

There were. The first ones she found were salesmen, traveling men, in their late twenties and early thirties, well-dressed and friendly men, who stayed for a night or a week at the Winston Hotel and who could be found, over a gin and tonic or a seven and seven, in the Winston Lounge, just off the hotel lobby.

But these men, too, proved finally unsatisfactory. After the first pleasure of bodily release, bodily gratification, she soon saw that these pleasant, polished young men were merely older and subtler versions of high school boys. She still had not been taken completely, not entirely. Where in Winston could she find a man?

A summer spent at a summer theater was a disappointment. Actors, she had hoped, would have greater depth and greater sensitivity. Perhaps they had, but these qualities were hidden by a greater egotism. The men she met in the summer theater were so completely interested in themselves that they had neither the time nor the ability to be really interested in her.

Now she was eighteen, and a junior in college. She had slept in any number of beds, with any number of men, but she had never been possessed, and she craved possession. The news that a novelist, Daniel Blake, was joining the faculty of the college, gave her hope again. A writer, and a young and handsome one at that. He should share the sensitivity of the actor, but without the actor's self interest. She signed for his writing course at once, though she had never had even the slightest interest in writing. When she met Blake, on registration day, she was not disappointed. He was impersonal, of course, he would have to be. There was a student-teacher relationship to be gotten out of the way, but that shouldn't be too difficult. They chatted for about fifteen minutes, during registration, mainly concerning books she had read and enjoyed, and then someone else interrupted, someone else registering for the writing course. Janice had left gracefully, smiling at Blake, hating the someone else.

She knew she would have to move slowly, that Blake would be too smart and too cautious to want to risk his teaching career by getting involved with a student. But she had patience, and skill, and need. Things would work out.

Her registration complete, she left the gymnasium and walked across the campus to the student parking lot. People she knew, boys and girls, all boring, waved and called to her and she answered them without thinking. She got behind the wheel of her convertible, a powder blue 1956 Oldsmobile, a high school graduation present from Daddy, and drove back toward town, thinking about Daniel Blake. She drove with the convertible top down, the wind cool on her flushed cheeks, and she felt excited and happy.

She would have to get rid of Annette, first thing. She was so sure, this time, so positive that Blake was the man she had been looking for, that she no longer felt any need for Annette. Annette was the town whore, a pale and fragile girl who hated men, silently, and served men, silently. How she had started in whoredom, or why she stayed, Janice could never find out. But these two contradictory facts she did know; Annette hated men, and Annette was a whore.

Janice had known Annette for two years now, and they made a strange pair. Annette loved Janice because a woman who hates men had no one left to love but women. And Janice accepted Annette's love because she needed someone, something, while she was waiting for a man who was more than the over-eager boys, the placid businessmen, the shallow traveling men or the self-centered actors. And now she had found one, she was sure of it, and she didn't need Annette any longer.

It would be difficult to tell Annette, of course. Janice sped along the highway toward town, her loafered foot pressing the accelerator as she tried to think of what she would say to Annette, how she would make the break clean and complete.

Finally, she decided to simply stay away from Annette, avoid her completely. Maybe Annette would get the idea, and look for some other girl to rub away the caresses of men. Janice had told her from the very beginning that their arrangement could only be temporary, that she herself was no lesbian, that Annette was only useful until Janice had found a man.

Reaching the Winston turn-off, she decelerated slightly and whipped around the long curve to the town road. Once in town, she drove straight to the library. She really should read Daniel Blake's book. It would give them something to talk about, while they were getting to know each other.

By two o'clock Thursday afternoon, when the writing class met for the first time, she had read the book twice. The first time, she read rapidly, for the story only. The second time, she read carefully, looking for those characters and sections and scenes that she thought the author himself most particularly liked. They would be her favorite, too.

Thursday's class was a disappointment. Blake was formal and impersonal, and just a bit nervous. He informed them that the course would be a writing course, not a reading course, so there would be no textbooks. He spoke a little, generally, without saying anything, and dismissed the class, having given no assignment.

While Blake droned on, Janice studied the seven other students in the class. The three girls were all innocuous, each in her own way. One was a peaches-and-cream, pony tail, flower print dress, simpering and insipid girl-next-door type. One was a baggy tweed skirt, shapeless brown sweater, straight hair, thick eyeglasses, humorless, intelligent, sincere type. And the third, dressed all in black, her black hair short and scrambled, was trying her damnedest to be a Beatnik.

The four male students weren't much better. Of them all, only Dave Markham was in any way disturbing. She might have known Dave would be in this class, he had played at being a writer since way back in high school, had even sold a silly little science fiction story a few months back. Dave looked over at her when she came into the class, a sardonic smile on his pimply face, his eyes leering at her behind his spectacles. Dave had always made her nervous. They had met as high school freshmen, and had disliked each other from the very first. He always looked at her in that same leering, sarcastic manner, as though he knew some dirty secret about her. She knew the expression was only defensive, that he used it to hide his own insecurity, but it made her nervous nevertheless. She couldn't help wondering whether he really did know something. About Annette? Or the salesmen at the hotel, while she was a high school senior? Or something else?

She ignored him during class, but she didn't move fast enough when Blake dismissed them, half an hour early. Dave was at her side before she reached the door. "Give me a ride to town?" he asked her.

She thought of telling him that she wasn't going to town yet, she had another class or some other thing, but he would know she was lying, and that he made her nervous. "All right," she said, and moved swiftly down the corridor toward the exit, leaving him to follow her.

He caught up with her outside, and they walked silently across the campus toward the student parking lot. Dave was lugging a pile of textbooks, and Janice knew it was affectation.

This was only the second day of class, he couldn't possibly need all those books yet.

They got into the Oldsmobile, Dave tossing his books onto the back seat, and Janice drove off the campus. As they turned left onto the highway, Dave said, casually, as though just making conversation, "What do you think of Blake?"

"He's all right, I guess," she said. "It's too early to tell."

Dave laughed, and she looked over at him. He had that knowing expression on his face again. "Forget it," he said.

"What?"

"You know what I mean. And you can just forget it."

"I don't know what you mean at all," She glared at the highway, refusing to look at him again.

"Sure you do," he said. She could tell from his voice that he was grinning. "Sure you do. And you can just forget it. You know why?"

She compressed her lips, not answering him.

"Okay," he said. "If you don't want to know, I won't tell you."

"I don't even know what you're talking about," she said.

He laughed at her, enjoying her discomfort. "What do you think of the new girls' gym teacher?"

"I didn't even know there was one." She couldn't figure this part out. What was he leading up to?

"Her name's Shallcross," Dave told her. "*Miss* Shallcross. She has the apartment next to Blake."

"So what?"

"So you can just forget it," he said again. "She got there first. They went to the Blue Room together last night."

"How do you know? Did you follow them?"

"No," he said easily, not offended at all. "I just happened to see them there. I had a date."

"Who'd go out with you?"

But he wouldn't get angry. "On the way back to town," he said, "I saw Blake's car parked at the old campus."

"What's that got to do with me?"

"Nothing," he said. "That's what I've been telling you. Blake has nothing to do with you. So you can just forget the whole thing."

"What did you think, I was going to make a play for him? Don't be silly. He's a teacher, and I'm a student."

Dave laughed again. "How long you been interested in writing?" he asked her.

"For years."

They were coming into town now. "Let me off at the next corner, okay? I've got some business downtown."

She stopped the car, happy to be rid of him. He fumbled around in the back seat for a minute, collecting his books, then climbed out of the car. He held the door open and grinned at her. "Blake doesn't know how lucky he is, does he?" he asked. "What a close call he had."

"Your mind ought to be washed out with soap," she said.

He laughed gaily, and closed the door. She drove away, seeing him in the rearview mirror, standing at the curb and smiling at her.

She was boiling mad by the time she got home and, to make matters worse, there had been a call from Annette. Her mother was in the living room, watching television, and when Janice came in she said, "Honey, some girl called for you a little while ago. I wrote the number down on the pad."

"Who was it, did she say?"

"I'm not sure. Sally, or Sandra, or something like that."

Janice went to the telephone stand in the dining room and looked at the pad. The name given was Susan, but it was Annette's phone number. Janice hadn't wanted Annette to call the house at all, but had compromised finally when Annette's insistence grew tearful. Annette could call, but she couldn't use her right name.

Now what to do? Ignore the call? But if Dave was right about Blake and the gym teacher, it might take a long while to get Blake for herself. She never for a minute doubted that she could get Blake eventually. But the gym teacher might make the process more difficult, much slower. In the meantime, Annette would still be needed. She decided, finally, and dialed Annette's number.

The faint, frail voice came on at last, and Janice said, "Susan? Hi. Mother told me you'd called."

"Janice!" breathed Annette, and Janice had the irritated feeling that Annette was about to burst into tears. "Where've you been, Honey?"

"Opening of school, you know," she said. "I've been pretty busy the last few days."

"Honey," whined Annette, "I've been waiting and waiting. Can you come over now? Just for a little while."

"We'll be eating supper pretty soon," Janice told her. Through the archway, she could see her mother, sitting in an easy chair, her feet up on a hassock, watching the television set and listening to her daughter's phone conversation. Janice had to be careful with her wording. "I can't leave the house now."

"After supper." Annette's voice broke with pleading. "I'll be here all evening, I'll tell Jerry I'm just not going to work."

"I do have studying to do."

"Just for a little while, honey, please. I haven't seen you for days."

"I don't think I could," said Janice. She wished her mother would go out to the kitchen and do something about dinner, or go anywhere for that matter, so she could talk to Annette, calm her down, shut her up and get rid of her, at least for the time being.

Annette's voice had climbed to a wailing by now. "Janice, I can't stand it! I've got to see you, I'll come over there to see you—"

"Don't you dare!" Janice had forgotten herself and raised her voice, and she saw her mother looking around at her with surprise. She thought desperately. "I want to see that movie, too," she said quickly. "Don't you dare go without me." She looked at her mother, then, and said, "Supper at six?"

"A little late tonight, dear. Your father won't be home until almost six."

"Okay." Turning back to the phone, she said, "I'll pick you up at your place a little after seven, and we'll go to the early show. All right?"

"All right, honey, fine. I'll wait right here." Annette was almost giggling now that she knew Janice would come to see her after all.

"I'll see you then," said Janice, and hung up. She went upstairs wearily, and walked into her bedroom, where she sat on the edge of the bed and tried to think. It hadn't occurred to her that it would be difficult to get rid of Annette, but now that she thought about it, she could see where it might be very difficult indeed. Annette, if she put her mind to it, could cause a lot of trouble. Janice wasn't sure what to do, right now. The thing was, she couldn't trust Dave. He might have been lying, just to get a rise out of her. No, she couldn't do anything about Annette until she knew for sure what the situation was with Blake. Damn Dave Markham anyway! And damn whatever-her-name-was, the gym teacher. And damn Annette, too, because she would be troublesome sooner or later, Janice realized that now, and realized she should never have let the relationship get as deep as it had.

She was silent all through dinner, lost in her own thoughts, as her father rambled on about some property sale for the new television station. Her father was an attorney, with a very comfortable income, who had made his money by staying out of courts. His clients were corporations and merchants and businessmen, and every dinnertime he droned away about contracts and partnerships and bank-ruptcies, while Janice's mother listened with rapt attention, loving every word of it. Janice was only bored, and turned her ears off, ignoring the words and hearing only the droning.

Supper was finished, finally, and mother said, "Have a good time at the movies, dear."

"I will, Mother," said Janice, and left the house.

It took a while to get to Annette's house. She lived on the other side of town, and Janice had to drive through the main business section. Since the stores were open till nine on Thursday nights, traffic was hopelessly snarled in the down-town area. Janice waited irritably and impatiently for the line of cars to get moving.

Annette was waiting on her front porch, and hurried down to the curb when she saw the blue Oldsmobile coming. Janice stopped just long enough for Annette to climb in, then drove rapidly away from the house. They had a reciprocal arrangement. Annette was never to meet or talk to Janice's parents, and Janice was to stay away from Annette's mother (her father had disappeared when she was six) and "Uncle" Jerry, the cabdriver who brought Annette her customers.

They drove out of town, to the dirt road where Annette had been with Blake, and on the way Annette talked constantly. "I'm sorry, Janice," she said, her thin face plaintive, "I'm sorry I called you. But I hadn't seen you in I don't know how long, and I was afraid you were mad at me or something."

"Four days," said Janice.

"It seemed longer, honey, it really did." Annette reached out timidly to touch Janice's knee. "It seemed like forever," she said.

"Don't touch me while I'm driving."

Annette pulled her hand back. "I'm sorry. You are mad, aren't you?"

"No, I'm not mad. I'm just thinking, that's all."

"Don't be mad at me, honey. I love you so much, I can't bear to be away from you, not for even a minute." She smiled suddenly, and the smile looked strange and forlorn on her pale, thin face. "Don't you wish we could just go away?" she asked. "Don't you, Janice? We could just go away, just keep on driving, and go anywhere we wanted and not worry about anybody or anything at all."

"Except money," said Janice.

"I could work," said Annette. "Same as I'm doing here. I'd make good money." She was excited by the idea now, and talked about it as though it were something they could really do together. "We could go to New York or somewhere," she said. "I could support us both, easy, and we could have an apartment together and everything. Wouldn't that be wonderful, honey? Just the two of us."

"Sure," said Janice. She was only half listening, thinking about Blake and Dave Markham and the gym teacher, trying to ignore the whining voice from beside her.

"Let's do it!" Annette leaned forward, her eyes bright with excitement. "Let's do it right now. We won't stop for anything, won't pack or anything at all. We'll just keep driving, go over to New York or Boston or someplace. We could, honey. What do you say? Janice?"

Janice glanced over at her, annoyed. "What? Don't be silly."

"We could, honey! Why couldn't we? Honey, Janice, please, let's just go away from here. We'll be happy together, and I can work—"

A red light stopped them, and Janice looked at Annette, letting the annoyance show on her face. "Just how far do you think we'd get?" she demanded. "How far before my father started looking for us? Or Jerry?"

"They'd never find us. Not if we went to a big city, like New York or somewhere."

"My father would find us," said Janice. "He'd hire private detectives, he'd put out a ten-state alarm. He'd find us. And didn't you tell me Jerry used to live in New York? He'd find us, too, in his own way."

"We wouldn't have to go to New York."

A car behind them sounded its horn, and Janice looked up to see that the light was green. She drove across the intersection, and Annette said, "We could go somewhere else. To California, maybe."

"Where do we get all this money?" Janice asked her.

"I told you, I could work."

"Sure. You start streetwalking in a strange town, and you'll be in jail the very first day."

"We could work it out, honey." Annette was pleading again, the smile gone from her face, pleading with Janice to help her keep the dream going for a while longer. "We'd have each other," she whined. "We'd be all right, it would work out."

"It's a lot of nonsense," said Janice flatly. "I know you're stupid, but I didn't know you were *that* stupid."

Annette subsided then into a hurt silence, as they drove the rest of the way out of town. Janice turned off when they reached the dirt road and stopped when they were far enough from the highway. It was just beginning to get dark, and in the early evening gloom, Annette looked like a helpless and mistreated child, huddled in the corner of the front seat. Janice felt a kind of irritated pity. "I'm sorry, Annette," she said. "I was thinking about things. But it isn't a good idea, honey, it just wouldn't work."

"If you say so," said Annette, in a small and defeated voice.

"Oh, come on, honey, cheer up. Hey, is it getting chilly?"

"A little, I guess."

"I'll put the top up." Janice started the engine again, and the convertible top lifted over them. She hooked it into place and turned the motor off. "There," she said. "That's cozier, isn't it?"

"I wish we could go away together," said Annette. She looked up the way a dog looks at a cruel master. "I love you, Janice," she said.

"I love you, too," said Janice mechanically. It occurred to her that their positions were reversed, just the opposite of what they should be. Annette was the lesbian, and Janice was definitely not a lesbian. But Annette was the weaker of the two, the more fragile and womanish, while Janice was strong. In their relationship, Annette was always the passive partner, receiving Janice's attentions, and Janice was always the aggressor.

It had never occurred to her before. And now she thought about it, she always did feel some sort of excitement whenever she was alone with Annette like this. The thought of touching that thin body, kissing it, always aroused her, and she played the man's part when they made love together. She didn't feel that same excitement tonight, and its absence made her more aware of it. She knew why she didn't feel excited about Annette. She was thinking about Blake, she was beginning the job of transferring her sexual appetites from Annette to Blake, and Annette was no longer necessary to her. Which proved that she wasn't a lesbian, even though she did take the man's part. That proved it. And she was surprised, and just a little worried, that she had had to prove it to herself. Oh, it was time to get rid of Annette, there was no question about that. And the sooner the better.

"What's wrong, honey?" Annette was asking. Her hand was on Janice's knee again, and she was leaning forward, peering with worried concern into Janice's eyes.

"Nothing, dear," said Janice. She put her arm around the other girl's thin shoulders, and smiled at her. "I'm all right now."

Annette came into her arms and they kissed. Janice moved her hands over Annette's body, stripping her clothing away, fondling her breasts and rubbing against her trembling belly, all the movements they were both used to, but tonight the movements were mechanical. Janice caressed Annette's body, and barely felt the warm and trembling skin beneath her hands. This would have to be the last time, she would have to write her a letter tomorrow, say her father was suspicious or something, that they would have to stay away from each other for a while. It would only be temporary, of course, she would say that, it was only temporary. But the time would go by, and after a while it would all have faded away, it would all die of its own accord. That way, there wouldn't be any blow-up, any scene, no danger of Annette going to see her father or mother, no problems at all.

Janice thought of these things as her hands absentmindedly caressed Annette's body, and Annette moaned and writhed beneath her touch as she would never do with a man. "Kiss me," she begged. "Kiss me, Janice. Kiss me all over."

Janice bent over her, and Annette lay back against the seat, her head back and her body twisting. Her legs moved, her feet shuffling spasmodically against the rubber floor mat, and her fingers twined in Janice's hair. She crooned and moaned and whispered, and Janice loved her with her tongue and her lips and her sharp white teeth. They clung together in a hot whirlpool, spiraling down, panting, and someone rapped sharply on the car hood.

Janice raised her head, terror stopping her breath, and saw two giggling boys, about eleven or twelve years old, staring in the right-side window at her. As she moved, they turned and dashed away, and she saw there were three more of them. They shouted and catcalled as they ran, and stopped to throw stones, and Annette clung to Janice, shivering with fear. "Who are they?" she whispered. "Janice? Honey, who are they?"

"I don't know," said Janice. "Just some smart-aleck little kids. I don't think I ever saw any of them before." She said this with relief, hoping her quick glance at them had been right, that they were strangers to her. What if one of them had been one of the children from her own neighborhood or her own block? It would have gotten to her parents sooner or later. Janice didn't even want to think about that.

"I was so scared," bleated Annette. "I was so scared, honey."

"It's all right, baby," Janice soothed her, stroking her hair, holding her bare and trembling body close. "It's all right now, baby, they're gone, they ran away." And even as she caressed the girl, calming her, relaxing her, Janice was thinking that this might turn out to have been a good thing after all, these kids peeking in at them like that. She could say that the word had gone back to her father, that he was suspicious, they'd have to avoid each other for a while, and Annette wouldn't question it at all. "It's all right, baby, it's all right now," she whispered, her lips against Annette's ear, smiling.

Now, she felt excited. The stimulation that had been missing before was present now, called to life by the thrill of fear when she had looked up and seen a face staring at her through the window. Now she wanted Annette, wanted to hold her flesh in her hands and squeeze it and knead it, kissing the red-brown tips of her breasts, rubbing and stroking her body and being rubbed and stroked in return, loving her and being loved in return. But Annette was still too frightened and too nervous. Her body was cold and when Janice moved forcefully against her, she raised her tear-stained face and whispered, "We better go home, Janice. I don't want to stay here any more."

"They're gone," Janice told her. Her tone was rough, and so were her hands. She clutched at Annette's body, and Annette whimpered. "They're gone," said Janice again, angrily this time. "Stop worrying about it."

"They're watching us, I know they are." Annette whimpered and stared out at the gloomy, evening-shrouded woods surrounding the car.

"Let them watch." Janice couldn't wait any more, she couldn't waste time in silly argument any more. "Let them get a goddam good look." She reached across Annette and pushed open the door. Annette lost her balance and toppled backwards out of the car onto the damp grass beside the dirt road, and Janice leaped on her.

"Janice, please, please—"

Janice knelt straddling her, and slapped her across the face, palm first and then backhand. She squirmed, stretching out on top of the other girl, kissing her harshly, and their bodies ground together, their naked breasts and bellies rubbing together. They moved in the inverted position of love.

It took Janice a long while to get calm, once they were finished and dressed again. They drove around on the secondary roads outside town for a while, driving rapidly, with the convertible, top down, the blue Oldsmobile roaring with shrieking tires around the curves, and the wind dried the sweat of passion on their faces.

Janice let Annette out of the car at the corner near her house, then drove home. The stores were closed now, downtown, it was almost ten o'clock, and she made good time getting home. She parked the car in the garage, next to her father's Lincoln, and went in the back door.

Her mother was in the living room again, still watching television. As Janice went through, heading for the stairs to the second floor, she looked up and said, "Enjoy the movie, dear?"

"So-so," Janice told her. "It wasn't as good as I thought it would be."

"That's too bad."

"The cartoon was okay." Janice hurried upstairs, smiling to herself. The remembered touch of Annette's hands and breasts and tongue warmed her body, and she touched herself on the tip of one breast, pleased at the feeling of it. She could see light under the closed door of her father's study, and knew he was in there, searching through his law books for some unethical legality. She went into her own room, switching on the light, and closed the door. It was a large room, with three windows facing the front lawn and two more windows facing the house next door to the east. In the room were a double bed, an upholstered rocker, a small desk and chair, a huge dresser and a vanity table with an ornate mirror. Janice sat at the desk and collected stationery, envelope, fountain pen and stamp.

She stamped the envelope first, then wrote her own name and address in the upper left hand corner, and Annette's name and address, large and clear, in the middle. Then she turned to the letter. It took a long while to write, and she threw away three unsuccessful attempts before she was sure she had the wording right. Then she got the letter ready for mailing, and undressed for bed. It was too early to sleep, but she felt relaxed and drowsy. She switched on the small television set on the dresser, turned off the light, and went to bed. She watched television for a while, then drifted into a pleased and dreamless sleep.

5

I T WAS TRUE. Blake and the gym teacher, Ann Shallcross, were having an affair. Janice saw them together, on campus, in town, driving by in Blake's rattling old Ford, and she glared at them furiously. She had mailed the letter to Annette, had screamed her way through one phone call from the stupid girl, which had luckily come when she was alone in the house, and now she was free of Annette, free for Blake, and Blake had tied himself to a brainless simp named Ann Shallcross. Janice sat smoldering in the writing class, day after day, as Blake droned on and Dave Markham grinned mockingly at her. She searched for some way to break the stalemate, get Blake interested in her, but it was impossible. Blake was impersonal in class, and unavailable the rest of the time. Janice raged, at a standstill.

The only thing that relieved her anger at all was the pleasant fact that Blake obviously didn't like Dave Markham either. Dave insisted on completing his writing assignments by turning in his adolescent little science fiction stories, and he managed to get into an argument with Blake, almost every day, about the worth of "commercial" fiction. Blake obviously thought Dave a pretentious upstart, and Dave obviously thought Blake a pretentious snob. Their wrangling was the only thing that broke the monotony of the class.

Oddly enough, it was Dave who helped to break the impasse. One day, in the third week of class, he suggested that the group meet, unofficially, at other times, beyond the three one-hour classroom sessions a week. They could meet at the students' homes, he suggested, and chat more informally, go off at greater tangents than was possible within the framework of the course itself.

Blake had agreed with the idea at once, and Janice realized for the first time that the impersonality and formality of the course had been bothering him too. The suggestion was made on a Wednesday. Friday evening, said Blake, at seven o'clock, for the first gathering. And he invited the class to his own apartment.

Janice drove home that day feeling better than she had felt in weeks. Friday evening, she would be in Blake's apartment. Friday evening, the student-teacher formal relationship would begin to crack. She almost liked Dave Markham.

She dressed carefully on Friday. She knew how best to accentuate her gypsy-like beauty. A golden metal band around her black hair. A full black skirt with a gold-colored belt. A white peasant blouse with a low U-neck and short sleeves. Black stockings and black high heel shoes, the shoes edged with gold. A dark red lipstick, a careful highlighting of her large eyes, golden gypsy circle earrings, a gold charm bracelet, a gold slave chain around her left ankle, and she was ready. She studied herself in her vanity mirror, spinning to make the skirt swirl out, and she knew Blake would have to see her, have to notice her, have to compare her with his sweaty plain gym teacher, and find the gym teacher a poor second.

It was a blow to find the gym teacher present. Janice arrived ten minutes early, hoping to find Blake alone, but Dave was already there, and so was one of the other girls. Both were sitting in the living room, talking with Blake. Blake stood up when Janice walked in and said, "Another early bird." He smiled at her. "Janice Winthrop, I'd like you to meet Ann Shallcross, my next-door neighbor."

Janice turned and saw the woman standing there, smiling. She was dressed in gray slacks and a flannel shirt with the sleeves rolled up, a flower print apron over both, and she was carrying a tray with plates of cheese and crackers and olives on it. "Hello, Janice," said the woman, in that phony friendship instinctive to hostesses. "If you'll excuse me, I'm playing housewife." And she circled around Janice and headed for the living room.

At first, Janice thought that Ann Shallcross's presence was an unexpected blessing. Put Janice and Ann in the same room, and what do you have? One, a dowdy, plain, unattractive hausfrau. The other, a vibrant, young, sexy woman. How could Blake help but notice the difference, and wish he could trade the hausfrau for the woman?

But as she saw how Blake and Ann Shallcross acted together, their ease with each other, the way they glanced at one another from time to time and let their fingers brush together as they passed, Janice began to wonder. Could Blake see Ann Shallcross as comfortable, safe, and Janice as garish and loud and dangerous? She'd made a mistake. She realized it now, and as the rest of the group arrived, and the conversation got slowly under way, she sat silently in a corner and brooded, only half listening to the talk around her. She watched Ann Shallcross, moving around the apartment as though it was her own, housewife-hostess, smug as she could be, as though she were saying to Janice, "See? He's mine, and he's going to stay mine, so you can just get your hot little paws off him."

Well, it was all right. It didn't really matter. She'd made a mistake this week, but the game wasn't over. Next week, the gathering would be at somebody else's house, and Ann Shallcross wouldn't be there. Then it would be a different story.

With a sudden realization, Janice knew that she would have to have the meeting at *her* house next Friday. Her parents would be out, they were always out on Friday night. Ann Shallcross wouldn't be there, and Janice would put on a display of domesticity that would make a Home Economics teacher look like a character from Dogpatch. With that decided, she smiled sweetly at Ann, who returned it with a puzzled smile of her own, and joined the conversation.

And the whole thing fell apart, just as they were all about to leave, a little after ten. "After Dave made the suggestion," said Blake, "it occurred to me that he and Janice are the only members of the class who live in Winston. The rest of you all live in the dorms, and couldn't very well hold meetings like this in your rooms. And it wouldn't be fair to Janice and Dave to expect them to house us all the time. So I guess the only thing to do is come here every week." He grinned at them, more at ease and relaxed now than he had ever been in class. "It's a sacrifice I'm happy to make," he said. "I think we've gotten more out of this session than we did from all the class periods put together."

Janice was frantic. "I wouldn't mind having the group in at all," she said quickly. "I was just going to suggest we all come to my place next Friday. You can't do the whole thing yourself."

"Of course not," said Dave, and Janice stared at him, the most unexpected of allies. "We three, Mister Blake and Janice and I, should take turns. It wouldn't be fair to expect you to carry the whole thing yourself."

"No, really," said Blake, smiling but insistent. "I enjoy having people here. Let's just make it a regular date, here every Friday night. I think that would be the best arrangement all the way around. What do you think?"

Janice wanted to argue about it, but she was afraid it would look suspicious, and she glanced over at Dave, hoping he would raise more objections. But he didn't, and they all left the apartment, clattering downstairs while Blake and Ann Shallcross, looking like an appliance ad in *Family Circle,* stood at the head of the stairs, beaming down at them.

Outside, Dave asked Janice for a ride to town. She wanted to be alone now, to be furious all by herself, but she shrugged ungraciously and said, "All right."

Dave was quiet until they were on the highway, and then he said, "Well, I did my best for you."

She looked sharply at him. "What do you mean?"

"Come off it," he said. "What do you think I mean? And why did you have to show up looking like the chief camp follower of them all?"

"Camp follower?"

"You look more like a whore than your girlfriend does." Dave laughed at the expression on her face. "You didn't think anybody knew about that, did you? I've known about it for months. And I know you've broken up with her, too. You were pretty sure of getting Blake, weren't you?"

"You're sick," she said. "Plain sick."

"I'd like to see you get Blake," he told her. "I think you deserve each other. I can't think of any tragedy Blake deserves more than he deserves you."

She braked the Oldsmobile to a sudden, jarring stop. "Get out," she snapped.

He stared at her. "Oh, come on now, Janice, act your age."

"Get out," she said again. "You and your filthy mind. Just get out."

"Listen," he said. "I want to help you. You're out to get Blake, and I want to help you get him. Why act like a little kid?"

"If you don't get out," she told him, "I'll lean on the horn until the state troopers come, and I'll tell them you were molesting me."

"Me?" He laughed, mocking her again. "I wouldn't touch you," he said.

"Only because I won't let you." She glared at him. "Don't you think I know what goes on in that rotten head of yours? You follow me around, stare at me, butt your nose into my business. Don't you think I know why? You want me, you simpering little jerk, and you know I wouldn't let you get me if you were the last man on Earth. Now, get out of the car!"

His face was flushed now, whether from embarrassment or rage she couldn't tell, and he screamed, "I wouldn't touch you, you pig, you filthy whore, you queer! I wouldn't touch you with sterilized gloves on." He hurled the car door open and stepped out onto the shoulder of the road. He stared in at her, shaking with rage. "How would you like your parents to get a letter about that other whore? Or about those nights you spent at the Winston Hotel? Or what you're trying to do with Blake?"

"If you did anything like that," she told him, "I'd kill you. I swear I would. I'd kill you."

He slammed the door, and turned away, walking ahead of her down the road, striding along with his hands jammed into his pants pockets and his head leaning forward as he stared down at the ground. For one crazy instant, Janice wanted to slam her foot down hard on the accelerator, steer right at his slope-shouldered back, crush him beneath the wheels of the car. But then she became aware of the traffic streaming by her, thin late evening traffic, a car or two at a time, but enough to bring her back to sanity. Dave was beyond the reach of the headlights by now, walking through the darkness toward town, and she slid the car into gear and drove slowly after him. When she reached his trudging figure, she stopped and leaned across to open the door. "Dave!" she called.

He plodded on by her, without looking at her. She called to him again, but he kept going. She turned off the engine, got out of the car, and ran to catch up with him. "Dave! Wait a minute!" She reached him, and grabbed his arm, stopping him, twisting him around to face her. His expression was glum and angry, and he wrenched his arm away from her. "Don't worry," he said. "I won't write the letter. Don't you worry about it."

He turned away, but she caught at him again. "Dave, wait a minute. Listen, I'm sorry. I was upset, and you can get so goddam annoying at times—I'm sorry. All right? Come on back to the car, I'll drive you the rest of the way to town. Come on. I'm really sorry."

She stood blocking his way, holding his arm and staring into his face, and he glowered at her. "I told you I wouldn't write the letter, isn't that enough? Now let me alone."

"Please," she said. "Let's forget the whole thing. I got on your nerves, and you got on mine. Now, it's all over, all right? We won't talk about it any more. Come on back to the car, and we'll forget all about it. All right?"

"No," he said. "It isn't all right. And I'm not coming back to the car. You threw me out, I'm out, and I'm happy out. Now get out of the way and let me walk."

"Now who's acting like a kid?" she asked him, smiling at him, hoping to joke him out of his mood. "I was acting like a kid before, but who's acting like one now?"

"I am!" He shouted it, and twisted away from her again. "I'm acting like a kid, and *so what?* Leave me alone, for God's sake leave me alone and get the hell back to your goddam shiny Oldsmobile and *leave me alone!*"

"Dave—"

But he had stepped around her and was stalking away. She stood watching him go, not sure what to do, and the moment of silence gave her a chance to get her thoughts together. What did she care what Dave did, anyway? Or what he said, or how he felt? She didn't care a bit, it didn't matter whether he ever got to town, as far as she was concerned. Good riddance, anyway. She went back to the car and drove home. Dave Markham wasn't her problem, Blake was. Blake and his gym teacher hausfrau. She had to break into that combination somehow, and nothing was going right.

And who did Dave Markham think he was, saying he was helping her? Did she need his help? Had she asked for his help? The more she thought about him, the madder she got at him, and the happier to be rid of him. Maybe he'd stay away from her now. Poking around, spying—How in the world had he found out about Annette? And had he told anybody? It was a good thing she'd broken with Annette, before anybody else found out.

She drove home and up the driveway, past the electric eye that automatically opened the garage door, and parked the Oldsmobile, as usual, beside her father's Lincoln.

She didn't know Annette was there until she had turned off the Oldsmobile's engine and lights and climbed out of the car. Then the too-familiar whimpering voice was there, beside her in the darkness, and the hands were fumbling at her arm as the voice said, "Honey, honey, I've been waiting for you, I couldn't stand it another minute, honey—"

Janice pulled away, staring into the dark, trying to see Annette. "What are you doing here?" she whispered. "For God's sake, I told you we had to stay away from each other for a while."

"I couldn't help it, honey," whined the voice. "I couldn't stand being away from you. Honey, I love you, kiss me. Honey, Janice, please—"

Janice pushed away the grasping hands. "How did you get in here?"

"Nobody saw me, honey. I made sure of that. We're safe here. Honey, we could get into the car, right here—"

"What if my father came out? Are you out of your mind? Get your hands away from me!" Janice backed away, slapping at the hands reaching out from the darkness. She was closer to the door now, and some light filtered in here. She could see Annette's face vaguely, a tear-stained blur. "We can't take chances like this," she whispered fiercely. "If you do anything like this again, we're through for good."

"No, honey, no! Janice, honey, let's run away, right now."

"Now you're starting that again."

"I've got some money. I got all my money out of the bank, I've got almost five hundred dollars."

"Now, listen to me," said Janice. "Just listen to me for a minute. I want you to wait here. I'm going into the house now—"

"Honey—"

"Don't interrupt me. I'm going into the house, and you wait five minutes. Then push this button here, beside the door. Do you see it?"

Annette's voice was dull and hopeless as she said, "Yes, I see it."

"All right. This closes the door. You wait five minutes, then push this and get out of here, right away. Go home and stay there. Don't you ever, ever come around here again like this. I told you how dangerous it was, my father suspects something already. If he finds out, do you know what he'll do?"

Annette was sniffling, a frail wraith in the darkness of the garage. "I don't know," she said.

"He'll send me away," Janice told her. "Off to some relative or somebody. And we'll never be able to see each other again as long as we live. Is that what you want?"

"No, no, honey, you know I don't."

"Then you'll have to stay away from here. We can't afford to see each other for a while." Janice forced her voice to
be gentle. "It won't be for long, honey. We'll be able to see
each other again, after a while. But we've got to be careful
now. We can't take any chances on my father sending me
away. You see that, don't you?"

"I suppose so," whispered Annette. "But it's so lonely,
not seeing you, never seeing you at all. It's been three weeks
already."

"I know it, honey." Janice put her arm around the other
girl's frail body. "Don't you think I feel lonely, too? But we
just can't take the chance. It won't be long, you'll see. Now,
I'm going to go into the house now, and you wait five minutes. Then you go home. All right?"

"All right, Janice."

"And don't come around here any more."

"I won't."

"All right. Everything will work out."

"Janice?"

"What?"

"Kiss me before you go."

Janice frowned. How had she ever managed to get herself involved with an idiot like this? "All right, honey," she
said, and kissed the other girl quickly, without passion. "I'll
see you as soon as I can," she whispered.

"All right," said Annette.

Janice hurried out of the garage and into the house. Her
parents were home early tonight, and her mother, as usual,
was sitting in the living room and watching television. She

looked up as Janice came into the room. "Did you have a good time, dear?"

"Fine," said Janice. "We all talked about writing and things."

"That's nice," said her mother.

Janice hurried upstairs, noticing that her father was in his study, as usual. Everything as usual. And that damn fool Annette out in the garage! Janice glared at her reflection in the vanity mirror. Why couldn't things go smoothly? Why did people always have to disrupt everything? It should be such a simple matter. Drop Annette and pick up Blake. But Annette wouldn't let go and Blake wouldn't be picked up. It was frustrating, and Janice hated to be frustrated. And with that snide idiot Dave Markham around, matters were just that much worse.

She turned on the television set and lay down on the bed to watch. But she didn't pay any attention to the old movie being shown that night. She mulled over her annoyances and her problems, trying to figure out what to do, and who to take care of first.

Annette was the immediate problem. Something had to be done about her. It was becoming much too plain that Annette couldn't be trusted. She would come mewling around once too often, and the cat would be out of the bag. How in the world to get rid of her?

And what about Dave? What did he want, anyway? She couldn't figure him out, she'd never been able to figure him out. He was spiteful and snide and unsure of himself, but why did he keep pestering her? And why did he want to "help" her with Blake?

No, she wouldn't even think about Blake, there were too many other things to be taken care of first. That was the hell of it, that was the almighty hell of it. It should be such a simple thing. She and Blake, and it would be fine, they would have a wonderful time together, he could be more for her than any man had ever been. And everything had to keep going wrong! Damn Ann Shallcross. Damn Annette. Damn Dave. Damn everybody.

She got up at last and turned the television set off. She started to undress for bed, and looked at herself in the mirror over the vanity. She remembered what Dave had said, about her looking like a camp follower. She looked sexy, she knew that, but she didn't think she looked like a whore. The neck of the peasant blouse was pretty low, showing just a bit of the upcurve of her breasts, but it wasn't all that low, not even as low as a normal one-piece bathing suit. And the skirt was full, it wasn't one of those buttock-clinging sheaths. Dave was just a dirty-minded little adolescent, that's all. She looked at herself in the mirror, reassured and pleased with what she saw. Any man in his right mind would be happy for the chance to get his hands into that blouse and up under that skirt. Any man in his right mind. She smiled at her reflection in the mirror, and gently laid the palm of her hand against her breast. Any man in the world would like to touch that breast, kiss that breast. Any man in the world. Including Blake.

She undressed slowly, watching the movements of her body in the mirror. She posed after removing each garment, looking with pleasure at her body. The blouse came off first, and then the skirt, and then the crinoline half-slip, and the stockings and shoes. She stood in her slip, lace around the breasts and at the hem, and smiled at herself. She looked like the heroine of some Broadway play, standing there in her slip. She turned sideways and looked at the strong line of her breasts, her flat belly, her hip and thigh pressing against the white material of the slip. She cupped her hands around her breasts, slid her hands down over her body, half closing her eyes in pleasure at the feel of her hands on her body. Still turned sideways to the mirror, she ground her hips, twisting them back and forth, back and forth as she stood spraddle-legged. "Look at this, Blake," she whispered. "Look at this. I could tear you to pieces in bed, I could swallow you, I could drown you, look at *this*, and *this*, and *this!*"

Slowly, still rolling her hips back and forth, she pulled the slip up over her head and tossed it away. She was standing now in panties and bra, her body writhing as she watched herself, smiling, her eyes half-closed, touching herself and whispering, "Look at this, Blake, look at this. You'll want me, and you'll get me."

She reached behind her, throwing her chest out, causing her breasts to strain at the material of the bra, as she fumbled with the snaps. She finally got them, and the bra fell away from her breasts, still holding its cup-shape, and she let it drop to the floor as she clutched her breasts and squeezed, closing her eyes, feeling the pressure of her hands and the firmness of her nipples against her fingers, and she twisted and sighed, rubbing her hands against her body.

Someone knocked at the door, and she stopped, staring at the door. Her mother's voice called, "Are you in bed, honey?"

"Going to bed now, Mother," she called back, hoping her mother wouldn't hear her voice shaking. "I'm just getting undressed."

"All right, dear. Good night."

"Good night, Mother."

Janice listened to her mother's footsteps, receding down the hall, and then she stripped off her panties, turned out the light and crawled naked into bed. She could feel the pounding of her heart, still frightened by that sudden knocking on the door. And she realized all at once that her forehead was damp with perspiration, whether from the interruption by her mother or from what had gone before she didn't know.

She lay there in the dark, breathing hard, and tried at first to go to sleep. But the passion that had filled her just a few minutes ago wasn't yet dead, nor yet satisfied. It grew in her again, and she thought about Blake, and the first time they would sleep together, she and Blake, in Blake's bed, in a bed like this. And they would both be naked, and he would touch her first, he would fondle her and caress her and kiss her breasts.

Yes, he would, he would, and she would guide him, she would tell him what to do. "Give me your hand," she whispered, and she reached across with her right hand to grasp her left hand, now Blake's hand, and bring it to her breast. "Feel me, Blake," she whispered, and Blake's hand felt her, stroking her body, kneading her breasts and rubbing her belly.

She closed her eyes tight, and she could sense Blake beside her in the bed. She smiled as she sensed him leaning over her, as she felt his hand caressing her, and she whispered, "Your sword, my cavalier."

She could almost hear his whisper in return, loving, amused, puzzled. "My sword? I don't understand you, Janice."

But she showed him what she meant, and Blake understood. The world was hot and silent as she dueled with Blake, with his unconquerable sword, and in the end he won, as she wanted him to.

Her eyes were staring shut as she squirmed beneath Blake's stabbing sword.

And after a while, she slept.

6

THE SITUATION REMAINED UNCHANGED for three more weeks. Dave Markham avoided her now, not looking at her when they were in class together, or when they were both in Blake's living room on Friday evenings. Ann Shallcross was always there, playing hostess, being sweet and unobtrusive, and Janice grew to hate the sight of her. As for Annette, Janice heard from her twice. First, a pathetic, scribbled, misspelled letter that Janice threw away half-read, as soon as she saw that Annette was whining on about running away together again. The second time was another phone call, Annette tearfully wondering why Janice hadn't answered her letter. Her mother was home this time, sitting in the next room and watching television, and Janice had a difficult time talking to Annette. She finally said, "Goodbye for now," and hung up while Annette was still talking. She waited around the house for a while, to see if the stupid girl would call back, but she didn't. Janice breathed a sigh of relief, and wondered if Annette was finally getting it through her thick head that she wasn't supposed to get in touch with Janice at all.

The Friday night sessions at Blake's apartment were uniformly boring, but Janice didn't miss a one of them. One of these weeks, Ann Shallcross wouldn't be there. But every week, there she was, smiling her greetings at the head of the stairs, and every week Janice smiled back and wished the stupid woman would drop dead.

Finally, on the fourth Friday night, something happened that gave her renewed hope. Ann was there, of course, as she always was, hovering in the background with a trayful of soft drinks and cold cut sandwiches, and Janice sat on the edge of the conversation, half listening and only rarely speaking. Dave Markham continued to be a thorn in everyone's side, and he invariably showed up with some pulp magazine which contained, he swore, one of the best short stories ever written. Blake had asked him to read one of the stories aloud once, and the rest of the class had proceeded to rip it to shreds, from the view points of writing style, use of symbols, characterization, depth of meaning and the author's purpose, but that hadn't stopped Dave. He was back the next week, with another undiscovered masterpiece. He himself had now sold a second of his science fiction stories, and he was obviously trying to raise the value of his own work by claiming literary status for similar works in the same field.

Oddly enough, Blake was closer to agreeing with Dave than were any of the other students, all of whom considered Dave's magazines beneath their consideration. But Blake, in principle, agreed with Dave's initial contention. Practically all great works of literature, claimed Dave and agreed Blake, have come out of the popular or commercial writing of their day. *Don Quixote, The Canterbury Tales, Oedipus Rex,* the works of Shakespeare, all were written with popular appeal in mind. Those who wrote exclusively for the intellectuals of their own day were almost invariably ignored by the intellectuals of later ages.

From this initial agreement, Blake and Dave drifted into opposite points of view. If great writing always comes from popular literature, claimed Dave, then we should look in the popular literature of our own day for the great writing of our own day. Trash that keeps company with greatness, said Blake, is still trash. And the argument continued, week after week, while Janice sat in a corner, bored with all the talk, annoyed by the yapping presence of all these people and most particularly by the eternal presence of Ann Shallcross, and frustrated in her attempts to get a relationship going with Blake.

Then, toward the end of the discussion on that fourth Friday night, Janice, half listening and half asleep, heard Blake say to one of the other girls, "As I told you when you were here Tuesday evening—"

Janice almost missed it. It almost went by her in the droning buzz of conversation. Then she realized what she'd heard, and she sat up suddenly. Tuesday evening? Who was here Tuesday evening? Somebody else? Were there now two of them she had to contend with?

She looked around wildly, to see who it was Blake had been talking to, and when she realized it was the tweedy one, the most sexless person in the room, she felt relieved and reassured. No, nothing to worry about there, Old Tweedy was no competition.

Then what was it all about? Tuesday evening? How had Old Tweedy managed to be here Tuesday night? And could Janice manage it the same way? Janice decided right then and there to be a good little girl scout and give Old Tweedy a ride back to town tonight, and pump her dry. Her name. What was her name? Marcia— Marcia what? Marcia Something, it didn't matter, the first name was all that was necessary.

Janice waited, impatient for the discussion to come to an end, and finally it did. Dave Markham, as annoyed as ever, collected his pulp magazines and stomped off down the stairs without a look at Janice. Janice managed to get directly behind Marcia Something, as they went down the stairs, and was just about to speak to her, offer her a ride to town, when it occurred to her that Marcia, like the rest of the members of the class, didn't live in town. They lived in a dormitory on campus. So now what?

Well, she had to do something, she had to find out what the secret password was that got Marcia into Blake's apartment on Tuesday night, and whether or not the lousy gym teacher was also present. As she followed Marcia out the front door, she said, "Good discussion tonight, huh?"

Marcia turned and blinked at her, smiling in her vague fashion. "Very good," she agreed. "I've learned more from this course with Mister Blake than I ever learned before in all my classes put together."

I'd like to learn something from good old Mister Blake, thought Janice. She returned Marcia's vague smile with a dazzling smile of her own and said, "He is a good teacher, isn't he?"

"Wonderful. And he takes such a personal interest in his students."

And the hell he does, too. "So I noticed," said Janice, and her tone of voice missed Marcia completely.

"You're awfully quiet during the discussions," said Marcia. They were walking slowly toward the highway and the campus, and Marcia didn't seem to have noticed that it was odd for Janice to be going to the campus at this hour of night, instead of going home.

"Well, I'm pretty much the quiet type," Janice told her. "I like to sit and listen. You learn so much more that way. Feel like a Coke?"

Marcia looked doubtful. "I'm not sure. I do have a lot of studying to do."

"Come on, it's Friday night. Let's live it up a little."

"All right." Marcia smiled again, obviously delighted to have someone take an interest in her and make a decision for her.

They walked across the highway and along the main campus road to the student snack bar. Janice brought the Cokes, over Marcia's flustered protests, and they sat down at one of the tables in the half-full snack bar. And then there didn't seem to be anything to say. Janice hunted around for a topic of conversation, something she could start talking about that could gradually be led around to Mister Blake's apartment on Tuesday evening, but she couldn't think of anything. And Marcia seemed to be content to just sit there and gurgle her Coke through a straw.

There was nothing for it but to ask outright. "I hear you were talking to Mister Blake Tuesday night."

Marcia released the straw and nodded, smiling again. "He's such a helpful person," she said. "And always willing to talk to you."

Well, that's good to hear, thought Janice. "Did he ask you to come over on Tuesday?"

"Oh, no. I've been working on a kind of short story in free verse form, and I've been having a terrible time with it. And of course you don't get much chance to talk about your projects during class."

"You can talk about them during the Friday night discussions," Janice pointed out.

"Well—" Marcia blushed, and giggled a bit, nervously. "I get awfully embarrassed, talking about my writing with a lot of people around. I feel so silly."

"Oh, sure." Janice nodded sympathetically. "I know just what you mean. I've felt the same way myself, lots of times. That's why I like to just sit and listen to the other people talk."

"I talked to Mister Blake after class on Tuesday," said Marcia, "and asked him if I could talk to him in his office sometime, or something like that, that I was having a lot of problems with my story. And he told me to come on over to his place that evening, we could sit around and talk about it over a cup of coffee."

"And you did."

"Oh, yes, and it was a great help. Mister Blake is a very perceptive person. He understood just what was wrong, and helped me make it right."

"Who served the coffee?" Janice asked her. "Miss Shallcross?"

"Who served the coffee?" Janice asked her. "Miss Shallcross?"

"No, she wasn't there."

Janice covered a relieved smile by drinking some of her Coke. Ann Shallcross, for once in her lousy life, wasn't there!

But what about next Tuesday? Or the Tuesday after that? Janice put the Coke glass down again. "Why wasn't she there? Where was she?"

"Oh, she has some sorority meetings on Tuesday nights. She's the faculty advisor for one of the sororities."

"They meet every Tuesday night?"

"Sure. You know how sororities are," she said, in a way that suggested she herself didn't know how sororities were, and wished she did know.

"Sure," agreed Janice. "I know." She looked at her watch. "Boy, it's late! I better get going. I still have to drive all the way to town. I'll see you, Marcia."

"Okay," said Marcia. "Thanks a lot for the Coke."

"Don't mention it," said Janice, and to herself she added, it was worth every penny of it. As she headed for the front door, she noticed Dave Markham, sitting alone at a table over in the corner, looking at her with that knowing smile back on his face. He had caught the sentence, too, then, and he knew what Janice Winthrop was doing chatting over a Coke with Tweedy Miss Marcia Something-or-other. Well, so what? She stuck her tongue out at him, though she knew it was a childish thing to do, and pushed through the door to the crisp outside air. It was late November and cold, though there had been no snow yet, and the sky was clear and brilliant. Janice strode gaily to her car, which she had left behind the faculty apartment building, delighted by the crisp feel of the air against her cheeks and the frosty steam of her breath. She looked up at the living room windows of Blake's apartment and saw they were dark, and that the living room windows of the next apartment, the gym teacher's apartment, were dark, too. Around back, the kitchen windows of both apartments also showed no light. "Have fun, Mister Blake," she whispered. "Dear, perceptive Mister Blake. Have all the fun you want. You'll be having more fun next Tuesday night. With me."

She got into her car and drove home. She passed Dave Markham again, standing by the side of the road and hitch-hiking, but she didn't even look at him as she drove by. She wasn't worried about him any more, him or Annette or any-body else. The game was finally going to her. She sang as she drove, feeling more buoyant than she had felt in weeks.

The weekend dragged on for years. She spent most of the time in her room, sitting at her desk with a portable type-writer set up on it. If she was going to talk to dear Mister Blake about her writing, she ought to at least have something written, some sort of prop to get the conversation started. She had done a few things for the course, little descriptive essays and poems with lots of rhyme and little reason, but none of them were worthy of special consideration. They were all high-schoolish, just barely good enough to keep her in the course. No, for Tuesday night, she had to have some-thing different, something special, something written just for that meeting. She giggled often as she wrote, and was careful to keep the finished pages well hidden, away from her mother's prying eyes.

On Monday, she was as quiet as ever during class. She was tempted to talk to Blake right then, and not wait for Tuesday's class, but she was afraid he would suggest she come over right away, on Monday evening, when Ann Shallcross would undoubtedly be present. Impatiently, she kept silent, and waited for Tuesday.

The class seemed to be three hours long on Tuesday, but finally dismissal time came, and the class stood up, gathering books and donning jackets, as Blake stood by his desk at the front of the room, stuffing papers that had just been handed in that day into his briefcase. Janice threaded her way through the other students, moving from her normal seat at the back of the classroom, and stopped in front of Blake's desk. "Mister Blake," she said.

He looked up, interested, impersonal. "Yes, Janice?"

"I was wondering," she said, hoping she looked bewildered enough, "if I could talk with you sometime, about— about a problem I'm having. A story I'm working on, and it just isn't working out the way I want it to."

"Well, sure," he said. "Do you have time now? I'm on my way over to the office, we could sit there and talk about it for a while."

"Well, thank you very much, but, I'm afraid I can't. Not right this minute. I've got the family car today, and I have to go pick up my father from work."

"Oh, I see." He seemed to be thinking it over for a minute, and Janice waited, afraid it wouldn't work, afraid he'd say tomorrow or the next day or the next day, come to my office, my nice little public office and we can talk it over, God damn it all to hell, anyway!

But he didn't. Instead, he said. "Well, what about this evening, then? I know you live in town, maybe you wouldn't want to come all the way back out to the campus again at night."

"Oh, I wouldn't mind, really." Just the slightest touch of feminine helplessness, now. "If it wouldn't be interrupting anything, I mean."

"Not at all." He smiled. "Say eight o'clock? At my place."

"Fine." She answered his smile, careful to keep her smile only friendly, only a student smiling at a teacher. She couldn't go too rapidly now, she couldn't spoil the whole thing, now that things were finally falling right. "I'll see you at eight o'clock, then," she said, and happily left the classroom.

Dave Markham was waiting in the car. He grinned crookedly at her as she got behind the wheel. "Getting anywhere, Janice?"

"You should know," she said. "You seem to know more about me than I know about myself."

"You're right there," he said easily.

"Who asked you along for the ride, anyway? I threw you out of this car once. I can always do it again."

"But you invited me back in, remember?" He tilted his head in a mocking bow. "I've decided to take you up on the invitation."

"Why don't you go crawl under a rock with the other bugs? It's wintertime."

"Going to be summertime tonight at Blake's place?" he asked her. "That was what you were doing, weren't you? Getting things set up for a little private tutoring tonight?"

"You know so much."

"Not everything," he said. His tone surprised her, and she looked over at him, to see that he was no longer smiling, that he was studying her with a serious expression that looked strange and somehow wistful on his face. "I don't know everything," he repeated.

"Why, Davey," she said, "what in the world is it that you don't know?"

"Why I keep hanging around you, getting my face slapped."

"I've wondered the same thing," she said. "But you haven't been getting your face slapped, don't say that. I wouldn't slap your silly face. Your pimples might pop and get pus all over my hand."

But he wouldn't respond, would neither get angry nor return to his irritating smugness. He stayed serious, somehow sad. "Which one of us started this, do you know?" he asked her. "Or is it too long ago?"

"Which one of us started what?"

"This sniping at each other all the time, insulting each other, making believe we hate each other."

"Who's making believe?"

He looked at her. "I am."

"Well, I'm not," she told him. "And if you're going to get maudlin, you can just get out of the car and find somebody else to drive you home."

"Janice," he said, "please don't go up to see Blake tonight."

"Why not?"

They stared at each other, and Janice was the first to look away. She almost preferred the nasty Dave Markham. Then he moved, motioning with his hands as though he were shaking garbage from them. "Oh, what the hell difference does it make! One more or less, what difference does it make. At least it's a man this time, that's one thing."

"You can stop talking about that, or you can just get out of the car," Janice told him.

He was suddenly his old self again. "Touchy?" he asked her, and the beginnings of the normal mocking smile were on his lips again.

She refused to answer him, and she was surprised to find herself relieved that he had gone back to the Dave Markham she knew and despised so well. She started the car engine, and drove the Oldsmobile around the curving campus roads to the main gate.

By the time they reached the highway, Dave was completely in control of himself again. "About tonight," he said.

"What about it?"

"There aren't any windows in the bedrooms of those apartments. See if you can arrange things so it happens in the living room, will you?"

"So you can watch, you little worm?"

"Of course."

"Sorry. The apartment is on the second floor."

"I'll rent a helicopter."

"Besides," she said, being as arch as she could, "you are just about as wrong as you can get. I am going to see Mister Blake tonight to talk to him about a story I am writing, and that's all. You just have a dirty mind."

He laughed at her, and they rode the rest of the way in silence. Janice drove him to his home, and as he got out of the car, he said, "Have fun."

"Don't worry," she said. "I will."

She drove home and fidgeted the hours away until it was time to leave again. She picked at her dinner, without managing to eat very much, and then hurried upstairs to dress.

Clothes were important tonight. She had to look just right, no mistakes, nothing wrong, everything had to go right. Dave's remarks about her costume that first week turned her away from anything too sexy. She thought about a sweater and skirt combination. Very collegey, she could look the part at least, when he first saw her. But she finally decided on a pale blue dress, fitted from the waist up, with a pleated wide skirt. The dress had a wide collar and a high neckline, but her breasts were outlined perfectly. With sheer stockings and loafers, she would look young and innocent, but she would still look sexy enough to get a man at least mildly interested. Beneath the dress, she wore neither panties nor slip, but only a bra. She collected her short story from its locked drawer, and hurried downstairs to put on a coat, say so long to her mother, and hurry out of the house.

She drove too fast on the way out, and got to the campus ten minutes early. It wouldn't look good to show up early, she decided, so she waited the ten minutes in the car, she checked her appearance in the rear-view mirror. Her only makeup was a touch of pale lipstick, and her face looked young and fresh, framed by the well-combed black hair. Satisfied, she got out of the car and walked around to the front of the building. She rang Blake's doorbell, and pushed against the door when the buzzer sounded.

He was waiting for her at the head of the stairs. "Right on time," he said. "I've got the coffee perking."

"Good. It's chilly outside."

"I imagine it is. Here, let me take your coat." He helped her off with her coat, and she preceded him into the living room. "You look very nice tonight, Janice," he said, as he draped her coat across one of the living room chairs.

"Why, thank you very much." She turned to face him, turning quickly so the skirt could swirl around her legs. She smiled at him. "It was awfully nice of you to let me come over here this evening."

"Think nothing of it. Sit down, sit down, I'll get the coffee. It should be ready by now."

She sat on the living room sofa, feeling a bit nervous, knowing it was stage fright and would go away pretty soon. She held the story on her lap, and smiled again when he came back into the room, with coffee and cookies on a tray. He put the tray down on the coffee table and sat beside her on the sofa. "There, now," he said. "What seems to be the problem?"

"It's this story I've been trying to write," she told him, looking pretty and helpless. "I have a first draft done, but it just isn't right, and I don't know what to do to fix it."

"Is it one I've seen?"

"No, not yet. I've been trying to do it by myself, but I just can't."

"Well, what seems to be the matter with it?"

"I'm not sure. Shall I read it to you?"

"All right, if you like."

"I was trying for something like *The Canterbury Tales*," she said, "only in today's idiom, and without any sort of story frame or anything." She smiled sweetly. "It's called, *My First Lay*." Without bothering to look for his reaction to that, she picked up the typewritten sheets of paper, and began to read: "The man who first made me told me I was some of the best tail he'd ever had in his life." She continued to read what she had written, a description of that time, when she was fifteen, when she had first gone upstairs with one of the salesmen at the Winston Hotel. Her description was as complete and as graphic as she could possibly make it, and used words which hadn't even been used by Chaucer. She read the whole thing in her sweetest, most innocent and most youthful voice, without once grinning or even smiling a bit. The stage fright was gone now, and she listened to herself reading, and out of the corner of her eye she watched Blake, sitting at the other end of the sofa and staring at her, and she read the whole thing from beginning to end. When she was finished, she looked Blake in the eye, and found there, as she had expected, complete confusion and just a trace of embarrassment.

There was silence for a few seconds, and then Blake stirred. "I see," he said. "Well. Uh, what say we have some coffee? Before we talk about your, uh, story."

"Fine," she said. "I'll pour. Sugar?"

"One," he said. "No cream."

She poured coffee for them both, and sat back, relaxed and amused, stirring her coffee and watching Blake. "This is, uh, fiction?" he asked her.

"Well, it's sort of biographical," she said. "But I did fictionalize it a little."

"Well, it isn't publishable, of course," he said.

"Oh, no, I didn't think it would be. I mean, I'm not that good yet."

"Well, that isn't exactly what I meant."

Janice adjusted herself more comfortably on the sofa, crossing one leg over the other, and half turning to face Blake. If he were to look closely, he could notice the absence of panties. She enjoyed watching his struggle to avoid looking closely. "What did you mean?" she asked him.

"Well, it's just a little bit—well, salacious," he said. "I don't mean you intended it that way, but, well, that's the way it came out."

"Salacious? You mean arousing? Exciting?"

"Exactly."

"Sexually stimulating, you mean," she said.

"Yes." He seemed puzzled again, this time by her constant search for synonyms.

"Were *you* sexually stimulated?" she asked him.

"Me? I don't see—I mean, what's that got to do with it?"

"Well, you said it was sexually stimulating, and it couldn't be unless it had stimulated you."

"Well, yes, I see what you mean." He looked away from her, and studied the cookies, making a very careful selection of the one he wanted to eat. "As a matter of fact," he said, still looking at the cookies, "I was stimulated, just a bit."

"Just a bit?"

"Well, a thing like that varies from person to person, of course."

"Are you still stimulated?" she asked him. She leaned forward, placing her hand gently on his knee. "Are you?"

He looked at her, then, frowning. "Janice, just what do you think you're doing?"

"I was just wondering if you were still stimulated."

"No, I'm not." He looked very severe.

She smiled at him, and her hand darted up along his leg. "Ah hah!" she said, staring at him, smiling at him. "You *are* still stimulated. I thought you were." She kept her hand where it was. "I thought you were," she said again.

He got to his feet, pushing her hand away. "Miss Winthrop," he said.

"Janice."

"Miss Winthrop." He stood in the middle of the living room, glaring at her. "I suppose you think this is all pretty funny," he said. "Come on up and make a fool out of the stodgy old professor. But I don't think it's funny."

"I'm not trying to make a fool out of you," she said, still smiling at him. She stretched languidly on the sofa, her skirt climbing high on her legs. "I'm just trying to make you."

"I think you ought to leave," he said. He picked up her coat. "The game is over. You can go back and tell all your friends how much fun it was, and how flustered old Blake got and all have a great big laugh over it. Come on, put your coat on. The fun's over."

She came up off the couch slowly and gracefully, her lips curved in a sensuous smile. "Dear Mister Blake," she murmured, her voice low and husky. "Dear sweet bewildered Mister Blake."

He shook her coat at her. "Come on, take your coat."

"Do you really think I'm just playing a game?" she asked him. "Do you really think this is just a joke, and I'm just trying to make fun of you?"

"You're too young to realize just how dangerous a little joke this is," he said.

"Why not teach me a lesson, Professor Blake?" She arched her body toward him, spreading her arms. "Why not grab me and try to rape me or something? That would show me not to play games, wouldn't it?"

He smiled frostily. "No, thank you. I'm not looking to lose my job."

She studied him, smiling and sure of herself. "You're afraid of me," she said.

"Are you going to leave, or am I going to have to throw you out?"

"You're going to have to throw me out."

"All right, I will." He strode toward her, his face stony, and grabbed her arm. She twisted toward him, wrapping her free arm around his neck, and pressed her lips against his. She squirmed her body against him, flicking her tongue against his lips. She felt him try to pull away, and held him tighter, clamping her arms around him, writhing against him, and gradually she felt him beginning to respond, and she knew it was going to work out, and he was going to be good, he was going to be very good.

His arms suddenly pressed her back, and his tongue filled her mouth, hot and burning, and she stood trembling, eager, waiting, as his fingers stripped away her clothes. She closed her eyes as he lifted her naked body and carried her to the bedroom, and when the cold bed sheet touched her back she pulled him down on top of her. "Stab me," she whispered, and arched her body to meet the sword. She pulsed, feeling the hot blood pounding through her body, the warm release flowing through her, and then it was too much, it was too good, too strong, and she couldn't move any more, she was rigid and tense, unbreathing, and it was finished, and the sheet beneath her back was hot now, and damp.

They calmed slowly, looking soberly at each other in the small yellow light of the bedside lamp, and Blake reached out to the table for cigarettes. They leaned against the headboard of the bed, smoking, relaxing, breathing shallowly, their legs and hips and shoulders touching, and she said, "It wasn't a joke."

"So I see." He smiled. "I'm not used to women like you, Janice. I didn't know there were any women like you in the world."

"I'm like Beth," she told him, naming a character from the book he had written.

His smile broadened. "You are at that. I thought I'd made her up."

"I wanted you to make love to me the first time I saw you," she said. "But you never noticed me, never paid any attention to me. That's why I had to do it this way."

"Why? Why me? Because I wrote a book? I've met women like that, and you don't seem like one of them."

"That's silly," she said. "It was just you. And I'm completely selfish. I'm very, very selfish, you know."

"How was it selfish? To make love with me, how was that selfish?"

"I thought—I knew, that you'd be better than any other man I'd ever had."

He seemed amused, and pleased. "Was I?"

"Not yet," she told him. "But you will be." She sat up, swinging her legs over the edge of the bed. "It's getting late. I have to go home."

"You're a confusing woman, Janice," he said.

She stood beside the bed, posing, the light gleaming on her warm damp flesh. "Do you mind?" she asked him.

"Not at all."

They walked together to the living room, and he stood watching her as she dressed. She glanced over at the window, a wooden rectangle framing the night blackness, a few dots of light in the center showing the campus across the highway. She thought about Dave, and could almost see him there, just outside the window, peering in at her. She knew it was stupid, but she turned her back away from the window and dressed hurriedly. "I have to run, darling," she said, when she was ready. She picked up her coat and crossed the room to kiss him swiftly. "I'll see you tomorrow night," she whispered.

"Tomorrow—?" He looked suddenly worried. "Uh, no. Janice, not tomorrow night. I've got too much to do here, papers to read and everything. Listen, I'll talk to you after class on Thursday, all right?"

She knew he was thinking about the gym teacher, and that what he really wanted was an evening to break off with her, so she smiled and said, "All right, darling. I guess I can wait another day. I'll see you Thursday."

She hurried down the stairs and around the building to the car. She felt wonderful, relaxed and easy, calm and satisfied. She drove back to town with the window open, feeling the crisp wind as icy needles against her face, and she smiled to herself. A man, again, another man, a new man, and this time she was sure. This was only the beginning, of course. Any man could have given her the pleasure she had tonight, if she were in the right frame of mind. But there would be more, she was sure of it. Blake would possess her as no other man ever had, possess her as she had always wanted to be possessed. In time. And now she had all the time in the world, all the time in the world.

PART THREE

7

BLAKE WATCHED THE GIRL skip happily down the stairs, wave to him, and push through the doorway, letting in a thin ribbon of icy air that slid swiftly up the stairs and curled around his ankles. He shivered, partially from the cold air, partially from the thought of the girl who had just left, and walked back into his living room.

She had left her "story" behind. He saw it on the coffee table, next to the uneaten cookies and the cold potful of coffee. He picked it up and read through it, realizing just how carefully she had worked on this little literary aphrodisiac of hers, and he sat down on the sofa to try to figure out what his attitude was.

Well, in the first place, he might as well admit to himself that he was pleased. It was very pleasant to have a good looking girl like Janice go out of her way to seduce him, it did fine things for the ego. Not only that, but she was good, she was damn good. He caught himself comparing her with

Ann, and finding Ann in second place, and he stopped that train of thought right where it was.

In the last few weeks, he and Ann had built a fine relationship together. They lived, most of the time, in her apartment, and they had fashioned a working household, a pseudo-marriage that was safe and pleasant and convenient.

Of course, there was little fire in the arrangement, little or no excitement, but that didn't really matter. They slept together, they ate their meals together, they shared their lives and their experiences, they could talk together, be comfortable with one another.

Until tonight, he had thought it a good arrangement. There were no permanent ties between them, and they had both made it clear from the beginning that neither was intending too force a permanent tie on the other. Once or twice, in the passion of sex together, they had said words of love, but neither of them had ever made reference to those words afterwards, when the passion had cooled. With Ann, he was content and comfortable and safe. Until tonight, he had assumed that that was the sort of thing he wanted. Until tonight, he hadn't even thought about it, hadn't even asked himself if safety and comfort and contentment were all that he desired.

Now, Janice had suddenly torn into his protected little world, and questions and doubts had poured in after her. Was Ann, after all, really the woman, the kind of woman, with whom he could be most happy? He had never seen himself, before now, as the safe and stodgy type. And, now that he was thinking about it, he did have to admit that Ann, after all, was, well, she was dull. After the first few times in bed, she had become almost routine, not much more exciting than a good dinner or a cocktail, and they had spent more and more nights without sex lately. How long ago had it been now? Three, four days. They were practically an old married couple.

It wouldn't be that way with Janice. Blake thought about her, remembering her in bed, and excitement grew in him again. No, it wouldn't be that way with Janice. It would take a long while for Janice to become routine, to become boring or dull. A long, long time, maybe never. With Janice, there would be a heady feeling of excitement constantly in the air, there would very seldom be comfort or safety or routine.

For the first time in a long while, he remembered the girl who had been living with him when he wrote the book, the first book, the one that had been good. Both book and girl, the one that had been good. She had been something like Janice, that girl, with the same quickness and liveliness and independence, the same aura of breathlessness and excitement. That girl—what the hell was her name? He couldn't remember, but it didn't matter, that was three years ago, the dead and buried past, she was probably married by now, and dull and safe, like Ann. But she had been the inspiration for Beth, the girl in the book, and Janice had compared herself with Beth tonight. And rightly so. Janice, the girl he had lived with when he had written the first book, the girl named Beth whom he had created in that first book, there was a toughness, an independence, a willfulness that all three of them shared.

The book. He hadn't thought about the book in weeks, wasn't sure at the moment whether it was in the office or somewhere here in the apartment. No, and he hadn't thought about his plans to write another book, either, not for weeks, not since he and Ann had first started to live together. Complacency, the routine, he was sinking into the quicksand of the mediocre and the safe, and he was leaving his plans and his ambitions and the necessity to prove himself, he was leaving them all behind, letting them all die.

He roused himself, got up slowly from the chair. Ann would be home by now, waiting for him next door, and he wasn't ready to face her yet. He had to think. This girl, this student, Janice, had suddenly forced him to think, and he didn't know whether he was grateful or not. He saw his reflection, pale and ghostly in the window, standing nude in the middle of the living room, and he grinned at himself. You've got problems, Mister Blake, he told himself. You've got some dandy problems.

And the first one was Ann. He knew he smelled of Janice, the warm musk of woman and of love. He would have to shower before he saw Ann. And by the time he saw her, he would have had to make some sort of decision.

He walked through the apartment to the bathroom, started the shower water running, and stood in the needle spray of lukewarm water, feeling relaxed and lethargic, his body ready for sleep. But his mind kept working. Ann and Janice, Ann or Janice. He had to decide.

His shower finished, he toweled himself dry and returned to the bedroom to dress. He still hadn't decided, and he found himself wishing that Ann and Janice were one girl, combining the qualities of each and removing the disadvantages of each. A cute dream, but not much help. Distracted and vaguely upset, he left the apartment and walked across the back porch to Ann's apartment, their apartment.

She was in the kitchen, sitting at the table and reading a magazine, a half-full cup of tea beside her arm. She looked up at him as he came in and smiled. "Hi," she said. "Problems with the students?"

"Right. One student in particular." He looked at her and noticed for the first time that she wasn't really very good looking. Pleasant looking, of course, but rather plain. She was dressed in slacks and sweater, and her body, with its small breasts and slender, muscular frame, looked almost mannish. Her face was just a bit too square, a bit too bony and firm looking, and her hair was, after all, rather mousy. He looked at her, and he remembered Janice, with the wild, gypsy-like face and eyes, the rounded, soft, warm body, and there just wasn't any comparison.

"Want some tea?" she asked him, and her voice was plain and matter-of-fact.

"I don't think so," he said. "I've still got some papers to correct. I guess I'll take it easy in the living room."

He knew then that he had made a mistake. Ann, teaching, the whole thing. It had all been a mistake. But now he was in it, in the middle of it, and what in hell was he going to do now? He wasn't making much money, and the Ford kept needing repairs. He'd only been able to save a little over a hundred so far. He couldn't leave, he didn't have the money to leave. Besides that, there was a contract he'd signed, to teach for the year. He had to stay here, for the rest of this year at any rate, and then he was through, he was finished with it. He didn't know what he'd do next year, but he wouldn't teach. Enough was enough.

There were only three more papers to read. He scanned them hurriedly, wanting to get them finished and out of the way, so he could go to bed and to sleep and stop worrying about things.

The last paper was Greg Matheson's. Blake remembered that first day, during registration, when Matheson had been fresh from the Army and full of spit and polish, the first student he met during registration, and what a shock it had been to look up at a bearded freshman well over six feet tall. Blake had grown to like Matheson since then. They both had a free hour after class, and they often spent the time in the students' snack bar, talking about one thing or another over a cup of coffee. Matheson was a serious, quiet type, despite his outlandish red beard. He was at the moment, uncertain of his future, but sure of his present. He was going to get an education, as broad and varied and complete an education as he possibly could. After that? Matheson didn't know.

Blake read Matheson's theme more slowly than he had read the rest of them. Matheson had a clear and concise writing style, and his themes usually showed some thought on the subject prior to writing, an oddity among freshman themes. It suddenly occurred to Blake that he could invite Matheson to sit in on the informal meetings of the writing class every Friday night. Matheson had never implied any leanings toward writing as a career, but that didn't make any difference. None of the people in the class, with the just-barely-possible exception of Dave Markham, showed much promise as professional writers. Matheson was intelligent and a good conversationalist. He would be a fine addition to the talks.

Which brought his mind back to Janice again. He wouldn't see her tomorrow, there was no class on Wednesday, but she would be waiting for him after class on Thursday, and she would be waiting for an answer. She would want to know whether or not he had broken with Ann, whether or not he was ready for a full affair with her, and he had to have some sort of answer for her.

If he told her no? What if he were to tell her that to-night had been a mistake, that he was happy with Ann—he could say that he and Ann were planning to get married. But what if he did? Janice was unpredictable, self-centered. She had obviously been spoiled all her life, she was obviously used to getting whatever she wanted. If he told her no, there was no telling what she might do. She could raise a hell of a stink, if she really put her mind to it. After all, he had slept with her tonight. And that had been a mistake. And now, for the first time, he appreciated just how effective her seemingly naive, seemingly childish stunt had been. Tell someone about it, her little method of seduction, and it would look like a joke, but it had worked. That was the thing to remember, it had worked, and Janice Winthrop was a little lady to watch closely. If he angered her, rejected her, she could get very, very dangerous indeed.

Somehow or other, he had managed to get himself into a situation that was dangerous no matter what he did. If he left Ann, if he started seeing Janice regularly, there was always the danger that they would be caught, they would be found out, and then he was through. And she lived at home, with her parents. If they had any sort of affair, it would have to take place here, right next door in his apartment, surrounded by the rest of the faculty. And there was Ann to think about, too. How could he drop her, how could he break off the relationship with her without her getting suspicious?

And if he didn't, if he stopped this thing with Janice before it really got started, then what? It was too much to worry about. He was tired and the hell with it, he had all day tomorrow to try to figure something out. He put the corrected themes and the classbook into his briefcase and turned out the living room light. He would decide tomorrow. Tomorrow he would be able to think more clearly, and he would get this whole mess straightened out. As he left the darkened living room and walked through the hall to the bedroom, he wondered just how this mess had happened in the first place. He had come here to teach for a year, to save some money so he could try again, try writing another book. When he had first come here, it had all seemed so simple. And now it was getting more and more complicated all the time.

Ann was awake, sitting up in bed, reading the same magazine. She had taken to wearing a nightgown lately, and the significance of that had never occurred to him before. But now he noticed it, and he realized what it meant. They were no longer lovers, he and Ann. There had been no ceremony, but they were now husband and wife.

She glanced up at him as he came into the room. "Get all the papers done, dear?"

"Just about," he said. "Still one class to go. I can do those tomorrow noon." He plucked wearily at his clothing. "I'm tired," he said.

"Christmas vacation's coming," she said, smiling at him. "Just keep thinking about it. Less than three weeks now.

"That's the only thought that keeps me going," he said. Stripped, he reached for the pajamas he had been wearing lately, then put them back on the chair and crawled naked into bed. He lay quietly on his back, his eyes closed, relaxing.

"Do you have any plans for Christmas vacation?" she asked him.

"Not at the moment," he said, his eyes still closed. "It's too far away. I don't really believe in it yet."

"I got a letter today," she said. "From my parents. They asked me to come home over the vacation. Would you like to come along with me?"

And there it is, he thought, there it is. No permanent ties, that's what we said, and there isn't a woman in the world you can trust. I bet you've got a whole timetable worked out, haven't you, Ann? I meet your parents at Christmas time, you meet mine during the between-semesters recess, we make the announcement during Easter vacation, and get married the beginning of summer, in June, just after school closes. I bet you've always dreamed of being a June bride, haven't you, damn you to hell. Aloud, he said, "I'm not sure, Ann. I got a letter today, myself, from a friend of mine in Maine. He wanted me to spend the holidays at his place."

"In Maine? I don't think you ever told me about him."

No, thought Blake, and I never will either, primarily because he doesn't exist. "He's just a guy I knew when I lived in New York," he said. "He worked for my publisher."

"My parents would love to meet you," said Ann.

"We'll talk about it. I'm pretty tired right now."

"All right, dear. I'll turn off the light."

He lay there, listening to the sounds of her, as she dropped the magazine to the floor, switched off the table lamp beside the bed, adjusted herself more comfortably beneath the covers. They were familiar sounds, sounds of home and serenity, and he was damned if he wanted home and serenity. And he was also damned if he knew what he did want.

Then he felt her touching him, her flesh warm beneath the thin material of the nightgown, and she rested one arm across his chest. He knew the signs, he knew what it meant. Tonight, for the first time in three nights, four nights, Ann was feeling the stirrings of passion, she was coming to him to do his duty, to crawl to her to make love with her, quiet the stirrings and let her sleep.

He just didn't feel like it tonight, he just didn't want to. Janice had satiated him, satisfied him, and made it impossible for Ann to ever satisfy him again. Not tonight, he thought, I'm sorry Ann, but not tonight.

He tried to pretend that he had already fallen asleep, but the pressure of her body against him was insistent, and now she had begun to move slightly, rubbing herself just slightly against him, and in spite of himself he began to feel just a bit excited. Her hands stroked his chest, and her breath was warm in his ear, and he lay still and silent, wishing she would just go to sleep, just leave him alone.

Her hands moved over him, caressing him, and her warm breath whispered in his ear, "Shall I take off my nightgown, dear? Darling?"

Desire swelled in him, surprising him, and he turned on his side, facing her, pressing his body against her. He kissed her, slowly, her lips warm and moist, and he forgot that she was plain and dull, he forgot that she was conspiring to marry him, he forgot, for just a moment, that Janice was so much better than Ann. "I'll take it off for you," he whispered, and his hands brushed her body as he stripped the filmy nightgown away.

She sighed and he knew her eyes were closed. She held him, her arms tight around him, and passion soared through his veins as they clamped their bodies tight together.

And in the height of his passion, he remembered Janice, he remembered the touch of Janice's body, he remembered the clawing, struggling brutality of Janice's love-making, and felt the passive, clinging, grateful body beside him now, and he closed his own eyes, closed his mind to comparisons, loved his Ann fiercely, wanted there to be no Janice, no complications, nothing but he and Ann, moving together in the dark.

When it was over, Ann slept, her breathing even and deep, but he lay wide awake, thinking. He was exhausted, but it took him a long while to get to sleep.

8

BY THURSDAY, when the writing class next met, Blake still hadn't made any sort of decision. He had admitted to himself that he wanted to sleep with Janice again. He had also admitted to himself that he was just a bit afraid of her, and that he didn't want to hurt Ann's feelings. On the other hand, he didn't want to marry Ann either, and if it came to a choice between hurting her feelings and marrying her, well, he'd just have to hurt her feelings and that was all there was to it.

He let the class take over the discussion today, and sat back to try to think, while the class talked about one thing and another among themselves. Once or twice, the class discussion got so far out of hand, with interruptions and raised voices, that it broke into Blake's thoughts and he called order again, setting the group off on a new and, he hoped, quieter line of discussion.

He had hoped that the class would never end, that time would stop and the seven students (Janice kept absolutely silent throughout the hour) would keep on talking throughout eternity, deferring his decisions indefinitely, but all of a sudden the hour was up and seven students were filing out of the room. Janice had spent the hour sitting quietly at her chair-desk in the back of the room, watching him with a half smile on her face, and she waited there until all the rest of the students had left. Then she threaded her way through the chairs and came to the front of the room and to Blake.

"I guess we have to talk," she said.

"I guess so," he agreed.

She was studying him, the half smile still curving her lips. "Let's go for a ride," she said. "We can't talk in here. It's much too stuffy."

"All right. That sounds like a good idea."

She led the way, and he followed her out of the building, where she stopped and looked back at him. "Shall we take my car? It's right over there, in the parking lot."

"We might as well," he said. "Mine probably wouldn't make the round trip anyway."

She was silent as they walked across campus to the parking lot and the blue Oldsmobile convertible with the black canvas top, and he was grateful for her silence. Every moment that deferred the question and the decision was a good moment.

They sat together in the car, Janice behind the wheel, and she drove the car smoothly and expertly around the curving campus road and out to the highway. They drove in silence, toward town and beyond the town turn-off to another turn-off and a secondary road on the other side of town. Blake looked at the stark winter scenery, the trees leafless and dead-looking, the ground covered with the decayed remains of the summer's grass and leaves, not yet covered by snow. He didn't know where they were until Janice turned left, off the secondary road, and the Oldsmobile jounced along a dirt road. And then he suddenly recognized the place. This is where he had come in the cab, with that whore, back at the beginning of the semester. He stared out at the half-forgotten road, remembering that useless and degrading experience, that passive, cold and bloodless whore, a happening that he had successfully stored in the back of his mind, as good as forgotten, where he didn't have to see it or know it was there.

And now Janice had brought him here, to this same place, this completely different woman. Though he had written nothing in a long while, his mind was still attuned to the writer's tools, parallel lines, irony, the use of symbols. He studied Janice's face, seen clearly in profile in the sharp late afternoon light. Her face was virtually expressionless now, as she concentrated on her driving. If she had any particular purpose in coming here, where he had been with the whore—what was the idiotic name that whore had given herself? Something French-sounding. At any rate, if Janice had any particular reason for coming to his place, it couldn't be read in her face.

They were coming to the spot, now, where the cab driver had stopped, where the small clearing was, just to the right of the road, where he had lain on the ratty blanket with the uncaring whore. Janice seemed to hesitate, the car slowed a bit, as though she were going to stop here, then it picked up speed again, and they drove on. Blake looked at the spot as they drove by, the flattened grass, the tiny circle of white off there in the weeds that was someone's used contraceptive.

He wished Janice hadn't chosen this place. How could he think about either Janice or Ann in a place that still reeked of his groveling with another woman?

The road curved away to the right, and he could no longer see the place where the cab had stopped. He lit a cigarette, a difficult process in the jouncing automobile, and waited for Janice to get wherever she was going, when he would have to come back to the present and make up his mind once and for all.

Janice did stop the car, at last, where the road curved around the edge of a hilltop, following the line of a ridge. Below them, to the left, a swift stream rushed among the shadows of late afternoon, surrounded by clogged bushes and weeds and an occasional tree. There was farmland, blurred and indistinct, in the distance, and the sun to their right, a bright, orange, winter sun, obscured now by trees.

Janice cut the engine and looked out at the stream. "I want to talk for a minute," she said. "I have something to say to you. Please don't interrupt me. You can talk all you want to when I'm finished."

"All right," he said. "I was hoping you'd talk first, anyway."

She looked at him swiftly, giving him a brief smile, and then turned back to stare at the stream again. "Tuesday night was a goal," she said. "From the first time I saw you, from even before then, I had that goal in mind, I worked toward it. I didn't think beyond it, not until yesterday, and today." She turned back again, not looking directly at him. "Do you have a cigarette?"

"Sure." He lit a cigarette for her, and she rolled the window down at her side, blowing smoke out into the cold air.

"I'm not in love with you," she said. "But I want to be. That part is up to you. But I want to tell you about me. I want you to know who I am first, before you say anything. That story I read you Tuesday night. It was the truth, or almost the truth. Close enough to the truth. I've been looking for something. I'm not sure what myself. All I know for sure is that it takes a man." She shook her head, as though annoyed at the way she was phrasing herself. "I don't mean I'm a nymphomaniac, though maybe I am that, too. I mean, I'm looking for something, I need something—it's more than sex. Sex is just a part of it, and I've never been able to find a man who could give me more than the sex part. When I heard that you were coming, when I saw you, I thought maybe you would be the one. I thought maybe you would have the sensitivity, or whatever." She laughed and this time, when she turned, she looked him in the eye, and she was smiling again, that pixie-like upcurving of the lips that was only half humor, the other half being sex. "I'm being too damn serious," she said. "I want you, that's all. I want you all, I want every bit of you, I want to chew you up and swallow you. Right now, I've only got part of you, I've only got sex."

"What more do you want?"

"What more have you got to give me?"

"I'm not sure."

"Let's get out of here. It's stuffy in here." She pushed the door open on her side and stepped out among the weeds and tall grasses beside the road. He slid across the seat and climbed out of the car beside her. "Let's walk a bit," she suggested.

They walked down the road, following the curve of it as it clung to the edge of the ridge. As they walked, she said,

"The reason I'm trying to be so serious and everything, is because of what's-her-name, you know who I mean."

"Ann Shallcross."

"That's right. Shallcross. You've been living with her, haven't you?"

"More or less," he said.

"Either you have or you haven't, and you have." She held to his arm, smiling up at his serious face. "Poor stodgy Professor Blake," she said. "I confuse the hell out of you, don't I?"

"You do indeed."

"Tell me about you and her." She stopped suddenly, in the middle of the road, gazing solemnly at him. "Tell me about your relationship. How deep is it?"

"Ann wants to marry me," he said.

"I don't," she told him. "And I never will. That's a promise. And what about you? Do you want to many her?"

"I've been trying to figure that out since Tuesday night," he said.

She giggled and executed a kind of dance step in front of him, a young and lithe and vibrant movement. "I exploded all over you, didn't I?" she asked him.

"You gave me a sleepless night Tuesday night, if that's what you mean." He grinned and nodded at her. "And last night, too. And probably tonight."

"And you still don't know what to do, do you?"

"You're right again. I still don't know what to do."

"I'll never marry you," she warned him. "I promise you that right now. If you're looking for marriage, you better run back to Ann Shallcross. I don't want any permanent ties at all. None of them at all."

"That's what Ann said."

She laughed gaily, and started walking again. "That's what all women say," she told him over her shoulder. "When they feel they have to, to get the man off his guard. The difference is, I mean it. And you know darn well I do, don't you?"

"And you know darn well I don't want to get married or have permanent ties either," he said. "Don't you?"

"I made a little guess," she said. She was still walking down the road away from him, and he walked along after her. "I made a little guess," she repeated, and did the dance step again, with a swirling of skirts high in the air, exposing her gleaming thighs.

Blake walked along behind her, watching the movement of her body as she strode along, young and strong and seething with sex. She looked so young and so naive walking there, and he knew that naiveté covered a shrewdness that could run rings around him. That "story" Tuesday night, that looked naive. And her conversation now, that seemed naive, too. He was beginning to understand her now, beginning to see the way her mind worked, and he had the feeling he'd been snared in a much stronger and more secure trap than the one Ann, poor little Ann, had tried to set for him. "That's a nice choice you're giving me," he said. "I can choose between you and marriage."

She swung around to face him, her skirt flaring out and wrapping around the swell of her legs. "Isn't that the choice?" she asked him. "Isn't that what it all boils down to?"

"I suppose it is."

"Of course," she said, grinning at him and weaving her body back and forth, stretching herself, "of course, you could always swear off sex completely, you know."

"I doubt that," he said.

"Then which is it?" she asked him. "Marriage, or me?"

"I really don't want to get married," he said.

"Blake!" She leaped forward, throwing herself against him, and her lips were hot and demanding as they rubbed against his, her tongue was a flame, her body was writhing against him, and then they were lying in the dust of the road, and she was laughing, squirming against him, crying, "My clothes! Blake, you'll get my clothes all dirty! Blake, Blake, you wonderful Blake!"

"We'll take them off," he told her huskily, and they scrabbled together on the ground, pushing at each other's clothing, unmindful of the cold of the air, unmindful of the clouds of dust raised by their squirming bodies.

And then they were nude, and they met, and moved together, holding each other with rigid arms and fingers. She clawed at his back, encircling him with arms and legs, and he felt drowned in her, swallowed by her, torn and buried in her demand and passion. It went on, and there was no time, only the spreading sensation, only the two bodies locked together.

And then they stopped, both of them at the same time, both rigid and tense, welded together, clamped into one. There was no sound and no movement, only the tension of their bodies and a draining, burning pleasure that was too strong, that was unbearable, and still the moment didn't break.

They were two again, hot and panting, smiling at one another, touching one another with gentle fingertips, feeling the cold air now against their sweating bodies, seeing the dust on their bodies now, and they laughed together. Without speaking, they got to their feet and gathered their clothes into their arms, and clambered down the ridge to the icy water of the swift-rushing stream. They left the clothes among the weeds at the water's edge, and both stepped quickly into the water, holding each other's hands as they waded to the deepest part of the stream.

The water came only to their knees and was so cold they could barely feel it. Their feet were already almost numb, and they were shivering uncontrollably. Janice moved first, kneeling in the water, splashing water onto her breasts, dashing double handfuls of water on her face. Blake followed suit, and then they waded back to the shore. Blake dried himself with his T-shirt and Janice used her slip, and they dressed hurriedly, both chattering and shivering from the cold.

They ran up the slope to the road and along it back to the car, and Janice started the engine and turned on the heater. They sat there, waiting for the car to warm up, and Blake said, "You realize we're both going to get double pneumonia out of all this. You realize that, of course."

"Of course," she said. "Wasn't it worth it?"

"Of course," he said, and pulled her over against him. He kissed her, at first gently, and then more brutally, and his hands rubbed her body, the curve of her thigh, the flatness of her belly, the firm coarseness of her nipples and the strong curve of her breasts.

After a while, she pulled away from him. "We'd better get back," she said. "It's almost six o'clock."

"I don't want to go back," he told her. "I don't want to go back at all. What the hell am I going to say to Ann?"

"I know, dear." She gazed fondly at him. "I know. It's going to be difficult. But you'll think of something, I know you will."

"I wish I was so sure. I can't just break off with her, I've got to give her some reason. I don't want her to get suspicious. We'd both be in a hell of a situation if anyone found out about us."

"You'll think of something," she said again, and turned the Oldsmobile around, heading back toward the main road.

They talked very little going back to the campus. She stopped the car just off the highway, near the faculty apartment, and said, "I'll see you tomorrow night."

"Tomorrow night? Again so soon? We ought to use a *little* discretion, after all."

She smiled pityingly at him. "At the meeting of the writing class, silly," she said. "What do you think I meant?"

"Oh, for Pete's sake, I forgot all about it." He grinned at her. "You've made me all rattled."

"Of course," she said coyly, "I may stay a bit later than anybody else, who knows?"

"I don't think you're going to get boring," he said.

"Well, of course not."

He got out of the car, carrying the damp T-shirt he'd dried himself with after the dip in the stream, and walked down the driveway to the apartment building. He unlocked the door to his own apartment, hurried upstairs, left the T-shirt hanging over the tub in the bathroom, inspected himself in the bathroom mirror, found himself halfway presentable, and went next door to tell Ann he was moving out of her apartment.

She was in the kitchen, as usual, standing at the stove. "Hi," she said, as he came in. "Where've you been? I've had a tough time keeping supper ready."

"I'll get washed up," he said, and fled to the bathroom. He wasn't ready to talk to her yet, he couldn't do it yet. He wondered if he'd ever be able to.

Unwittingly, she helped him. They ate most of their dinner in silence, but over coffee, after dessert, she said, "I was supposed to write mother today, to tell her whether to expect you or not. You still haven't told me, one way or the other."

"I told you about that guy in Maine," he said.

"Mother and father were hoping to meet you," she said, and her voice sounded, for the first time since he had known her, whining, with a nagging quality to it.

"Look, Ann," he said, "we're not married. You don't have any nagging license yet, you know."

"Nagging license? I only said—"

"I know what you only said." He was upset and worried, and ashamed of what he was planning to do to Ann, and it came out of him as anger, pent-up emotion finally finding a release. "I know exactly what you only said. I also know exactly what I only *never* said. I never did propose to you, and don't you ever forget it."

"Propose? Dan, what's the matter with you? Are you drunk?"

"Boy, if you aren't something straight out of Paddy Chayefsky," he said bitterly. He pushed away from the table, getting to his feet, and glared down at her. "The sweet little housewifey, for Christ's sake! Well, you aren't *my* housewifey, and don't you ever forget it!"

"Dan, what on earth—?"

"I'll give you your answer," he shouted at her. "I'll give you your goddam answer right now. No, I'm not going to go see your lousy parents at Christmastime. And no, you're not going to come see my lousy parents between semesters. And no, we aren't going to get engaged at Eastertime, and no, no, a thousand times no, we aren't going to get married in June. And no, I'm not drunk, but I'm going to be. I haven't had a thing to drink for two weeks, you practically housebroke me! Well, it's all over, it's through, it's finished, it's kaput, and I'm moving out. I'll be by in the morning to get my things, right now I don't think I could stand to look at you another minute longer without the two of us busting into tears."

Somewhere in the middle of his tirade her face had frozen, and she had arisen slowly to her feet. Now, she said, "You aren't going to have to worry about me busting into tears, Dan Blake. And you aren't going to have to worry about meeting my parents or marrying me or sleeping here ever again or anything else."

"Go ahead, Paddy Chayefsky," he taunted her. "Tell me you wouldn't marry me if I was the last man on earth."

The coffee cup glanced off the side of his head. It didn't cut him, but it stung, and it sobered him, cooled him from his frightened, ashamed, sudden rage, and he stared at her, gingerly touching his head with the tips of his fingers.

"Get out!" she screamed at him. "Get out, right this minute! And don't you come back, don't you ever come back here."

"My clothes—"

"I'll put them on the back porch, I'll pack them all up and put them on the back porch. Now, get out." She reached behind her and came up with a copper and steel pot. He got out—quickly.

It was done. He didn't know how he'd done it, or how it had happened, or much of anything else. All he knew, all he really knew, was that it was done, it was finished and over with and he was free of her. His hands were shaking and he felt nervous and tense, as though every nerve in his body had stretched to the breaking point. If he had ever in his life needed a drink, this was the time.

And, of course, there wasn't a drink in the house. He had bought some vodka, and a small bottle of vermouth, and a couple of brandies, but they were all over in Ann's apartment, and he couldn't very well go over there and ask for one of them now. At the same time, he did need a drink. He shrugged into his coat and left the apartment.

The handiest place was the Monequois Inn, next to the campus, where he had gone that first day, with Roger Kilbride. Blake strode across the highway, a highway almost completely devoid of traffic at this time of night on this day of the week at this season of the year, and walked along beside the campus fence until the fence ended and he was crunching across the gravel parking lot of the inn.

The bar, as usual, was crammed to overflowing with chattering, laughing, jostling, drinking students, and Blake had to force his way through, heading for the relative quiet at the far end of the bar. When he got there, he was surprised to see Roger Kilbride sitting disconsolately on the last stool. Blake squeezed in between Kilbride and the wall, and said, "Well, well, fancy meeting you here."

Kilbride glanced at him, then looked back at his highball. "Hello there, Dan," he said. He looked morose and

gloomy, and he poked idly at the ice cubes in his glass with a
swizzle stick.

Blake wondered what was the matter with Kilbride, but
first things were first. He waved and shouted until one of the
three working bartenders noticed him and came down to get
his order. Kilbride reordered while the bartender was there
and then, business out of the way, Blake said, "What seems
to be the matter, Roger? I thought you'd be home with the
family by now."

"Home with the family," repeated Kilbride disgustedly.
"Home with the family." He turned to gaze blearily at Blake,
who realized all at once that Kilbride had been sitting here,
drinking, for quite some time already. "I'll give you a word of
advice, Dan," said Kilbride. "Allow me to give you a word of
advice. Do not get married. Lie, cheat, steal, skip out of
town, even murder if it's absolutely necessary. But, no matter
what, do not get married. Take it from me, I know."

Blake grinned at him. "Little tiff with the wife?"

Kilbride studied him solemnly. "There are no *little* tiffs
with wives, Dan," he said. "Come to think of it, there are no
wives either. Only wardens. Keepers. Gimme machines. Do
you know what time of year it is?"

"November."

"Yes, of course, November, but I mean more exactly.
More precisely. But of course, you're a bachelor. This time
of year doesn't mean the same thing to a bachelor that it
does to a family man. You know what's coming pretty
soon?"

"You mean Christmas?"

"Exactly what I mean. Christmas. Did you ever hear the
expression, so and so many shopping days till Christmas?"

"Sure."

"Well, then," said Kilbride, as though that explained the whole thing. Then he amplified. "That's what we're in now," he said. "That's what we're right in the middle of now, *Shopping Days.*"

"I see." The drinks came, then, and Blake quickly ordered another round before the bartender had a chance to leave. He swallowed half his drink at once, then said, "So you had a kind of an argument about money?"

"I'm an ogre," said Kilbride. He poked himself in the chest with a forefinger. "You wouldn't think it to look at me, would you? Well, I am. I'm an ogre. You know what kind of ogre I am?"

"No, I don't."

"I'm such a despicable ogre," said Kilbride, his voice rising at every word, "that I refused to shell out a hundred and thirty dollars to get an American Flyer electric railroad train choo-choo set for a *five-year-old boy.* That's what kind of an ogre *I* am." Kilbride shook his head. "Dan," he said, "take the advice of a man who wishes he'd taken the advice of a man, and so on. Don't marry. Don't ever marry."

"I wasn't planning on it," said Blake.

"None of us plan on it," said Kilbride. "It sneaks up on us all. Hey!" He stared at Blake suddenly. "Haven't you been going with that Shallcross girl?"

"Used to," said Blake. He wondered how they'd gotten around to that subject.

"What do you mean, you used to?" demanded Kilbride. "She's a fine girl. What's wrong with her?"

"Nothing," said Blake. "I'm just not going to get married, that's all. I'm following your advice."

"What? Oh. Oh, pshaw, don't be silly, you didn't take me seriously, did you? Little tiff with the wife, doesn't mean a thing. It happens to everybody. Why, I'm going along home now, we'll make it up—that's the best part of an argument, the making up—then everything'll be fine again." Kilbride was struggling off the stool, grinning with embarrassment all the while. "I was just talking through my glass," he said. "That's all."

"I know," said Blake, smiling at him.

"Well," said Kilbride uncertainly, on his feet at last, "I better get home, I suppose. I'll see you, Dan."

"Happy Shopping Days," said Blake.

9

IT WAS THE FIRST TIME that Ann wasn't present at the Friday night meeting of the writing class, and Blake felt just a little lost and bewildered without her. When he had come back from the inn the night before, he had found his belongings piled helter-skelter in the kitchen, left there by Ann. She had returned his liquor, too, the four bottles were standing in a row on the kitchen table. He told himself he was lucky, he'd had a narrow escape, he was better off without Ann, and after a while he got to sleep.

After his three o'clock Freshman English class on Friday, he went back to the apartment and straightened things up as best he could, hanging his clothing back in closets, cleaning the place up a little, and then made himself some dinner. He was not the stereotype bumbling bachelor, and he was proud of the fact. He had lived alone quite a bit in the last three years, and he knew how to take care of his domestic needs without a lot of waste effort.

Janice showed up half an hour early. "I'll serve," she said, and headed for the kitchen.

"I'm not sure that's such a good idea," he objected. "They're liable to notice that Ann isn't here, and that you're taking over in her place."

"Don't be silly. I'm a member of the class. There's nothing strange about me being here."

Apparently, she was right. No one seemed to notice anything odd in Ann's absence, nor in one of the girls in the class taking over the serving of the refreshments. Blake had invited Matheson to the gathering, and he was embarrassingly grateful. The freshman courses irritated and plagued Matheson, and he felt obvious relief at joining a conversation that concerned itself neither with high school nor the Army. He had told Blake once, "*I* feel like a basic trainee again. It makes me nervous." He was rather quiet tonight, saying little, getting used to the group and letting them get used to him.

Matheson and Dave Markham and Janice were the last three left, after everyone else had gone on home. Matheson wanted to thank Blake again for having invited him, Dave was apparently ready to talk all night about one thing or another and Janice said, "I'll do the dishes." She winked at Blake, and weaved out to the kitchen.

Matheson and Markham finally left, and Blake went out to Janice, who was elbow-deep in dishwater. "Grab a towel," she said. "You can dry."

"We can do that some other time," he said. "Come here."

"First things first," she said. She kept on washing dishes.

"Exactly." He pulled her away from the sink and kissed her, and she grinned impishly at him, her soapy arms encircling his neck. "First things first," he said. He picked her up and carried her into the bedroom.

He didn't see Ann again until the following Wednesday, and then she avoided him. It was in the faculty snack bar, where he had started eating his lunch now. She came in just after he did, and stood to one side, looking away from him, until he was finished at the counter and was carrying his tray to an empty table. He was embarrassed at seeing her, and ate his lunch quickly, wanting to get out of the snack bar, where he wouldn't have to be aware of her presence any more. He wasn't sorry that he had broken with her, but he was ashamed of the method he had used. He could have been less brutal about it. He still couldn't figure out what bad happened, why he had suddenly flown into a rage like that.

Janice was coming to see him every evening, staying for an hour or two. They talked seldom, for there was nothing they had to say to one another. She came to the apartment, he kissed her, they went to bed together, and she went home. She was always laughing, always carefree, always exciting and desirable, but he knew there was no depth to their relationship and there never could be. He remembered what she had said about wanting more from him than sex. He was sure that she didn't know herself what she had meant by that, and he was equally sure that whatever it was, he wouldn't be able to give it to her. In the meantime, until she found that out for herself, sex was relationship enough. He was a transient here, a traveler passing through. When he left, he didn't want to take anything with him.

Each Friday, the writing class came to the apartment, but Blake rarely added his own voice to the conversation any more. He usually sat quietly in an easy chair, half listening to the talk around him, watching the movements of Janice's body as she talked, gesturing with nervous but still graceful movements, or as she brought coffee and sandwiches in from the kitchen.

Matheson had taken over Blake's role in the never-ending argument with Dave Markham. Matheson spoke easily, his rumbling voice controlled and calm, his red beard and high forehead making him look like some fantastic cross between a Viking raider and a German psychiatrist. He had told Blake that he thought now that he might go into politics eventually, and it struck Blake as a good idea. Matheson was calmly forceful, he spoke convincingly and well, and he had the appearance to back up his voice and statements.

Markham, on the other hand, had regressed in the last few weeks. He was now worse than he had been at the beginning of the semester, when he had been the most annoying, sickening adolescent outside a television family comedy series. He had been growing more human for a while, and Blake had allowed himself to think that he might have had something to do with the progress. But now he was worse than ever, argumentative, furious and infuriating, carrying on like the biggest spoiled brat of them all. Matheson had become his chief target, now that Blake was no longer active in the conversations, and Matheson's calm and control seemed to only agitate and increase Markham's fury. Blake wished there were some way to legitimately oust Markham from the gatherings, but it was impossible. Markham was a member of the class, and had to be put up with.

The Christmas recess finally came, and Blake had two weeks to himself. Most of the apartments in the building were empty now, the single members of the faculty all having gone home over the holidays. Janice spent some time at the apartment every day, usually arriving some time in the afternoon. It was a calm and pleasant and undemanding time, and Blake made the most of it. He ignored school, avoided thinking about Ann or writing or anything else, and the two weeks were suddenly finished, it was January, end-semester exams were three weeks away, and the routine had started again.

Janice had never became dull for him. Each time she came to see him, they made love together as though it were the first contact, and the experience was always new, always wonderful and always complete. With examinations coming soon, she showed up at the apartment less often now, coming only two or three times a week. The evenings he was alone he spent restlessly, trying unsuccessfully to read, roaming nervously through the apartment, looking out the living room windows to see if she were coming after all.

The first Friday after vacation, Dave Markham didn't come to the meeting, and Blake's relief was obviously shared by everyone else present. The discussion was calmer, more pleasant than it had ever been before, and Blake hoped that Markham would continue to miss the meetings, would never come to one of them again. He was quieter in class, too, a brooding silence, as though he was oblivious of the class around him, as though he were deeply absorbed by depressing thoughts of his own and nothing could manage to break through to him.

Examinations came and went, and Blake was kept busy grading the papers. As he had expected, a full third of the students in his non-veteran Freshman English classes had failed. A few of the veterans flunked the course as well, and Blake anticipated much smaller classes for the second semester. He had a more difficult time in grading the eight students in his writing course, and finally passed them all, failing none and giving A grades to none.

There was a free week between semesters, and it was during this time that Blake did the grading of the examinations. Janice stayed away completely the first part of the week, and Blake was too busy to notice her absence. She finally came to see him on Thursday, and she bounced joyously up the stairs, shouting, "Good news! Good news!"

He kissed her and, after a moment, she pulled away. "First the news," she said. "Wait till you hear!"

He followed her into the living room. "What's all the good news? You passed?"

"Just listen," she said. She beamed at him, pixieish and lively. "I told my parents I was invited to some girl's house over the weekend, and they said I could go. What do you think of that?"

"You're going away for the weekend?"

"Silly, what do you think? With you! Just the two of us. We can go to New York or up to the Adirondacks and go skiing, or anywhere you want. The whole weekend, all to ourselves!" She shook her finger in his face. "And we're not going to spend it here," she told him. "We're going to get out of here, we're going to go away somewhere."

"Are you sure? Your parents won't get suspicious or anything?"

"Of course not. I've got it all fixed. We can leave tomorrow morning. Where do you want to go?"

"I'm not sure," he said. "Give me a minute to think it over."

She was dancing around the room, happy, smiling. "Blake!" she shouted. "Let's make *love!*" She rushed to him, holding him tight, rubbing herself against him. "Blake," she murmured. "Blake, Blake, you wonderful Blake."

She was new again, new as always, a strong and surging woman body beside him, new and exciting and all there was in the world.

They spent the weekend at the Adirondacks, in a ski lodge, registering as husband and wife. It was the first chance Blake had had that winter to do any skiing, and they spent the days on the bitterly cold ski slopes, their nights in their room, a huge wooden-beamed room with a fire place and a mammoth bed, where they met again every night, as though it were the first time and as though it would be the last time. The weekend was all that Blake could have asked for, and it ended much too soon. And he didn't know it, but the relationship ended, too, when they came back to Winston and the college. From this point on, their affair was dying.

The second semester began as a repetition of the first. The Friday night meetings continued, and Dave Markham continued to stay away from them. Without his disrupting presence, the conversations were pleasant and quiet, and Blake sat silently, watching and listening, seeing the small group of students slowly finding themselves.

Janice was coming to the apartment less frequently, now, and her love-making was growing gradually less intense. They still did not talk, they still had nothing to say to one another, nothing in common but sex, and sex was apparently not enough for Janice. Blake soon realized that the affair was ending, that Janice would soon be searching with another man for the thing she had never found and couldn't define. He only saw her on Fridays, now, only made love with her on Friday night, after the rest of the group had left.

It was a Wednesday evening in the middle of February when Dave Markham came to see him. When the bell rang, he thought hopefully that it was Janice, whom he hadn't seen since the previous Friday. He pressed the door-release buzzer and stood at the head of the stairs, smiling in anticipation of Janice.

But it was Dave Markham, a subdued and hesitant Dave Markham, who stood at the foot of the stairs, small and vulnerable, looking up at him, blinking behind his glasses, saying, "Mister Blake? Could I talk to you for a minute? Do you have a minute?"

"Of course," said Blake. "Come on up."

Markham came up the stairs slowly, and Blake stood aside to let him go into the apartment. They say facing each other in the living room, and Blake said, "What is it, Dave? What's on your mind?"

"I've been a lot of trouble to you," said Markham. "I'm sorry about that." For the first time since Blake had met him, he seemed doubtful, unsure of himself.

"That's all right," Blake told him. "I understand, at least partially. You're young. We both are, for that matter, but I've managed to restrain myself to some extent. You will too, eventually."

"It hasn't been anything personal," said Markham. He peered pleadingly at Blake, and Blake had the feeling that

Markham had come here to talk about something else, that he hadn't as yet mentioned the subject that was uppermost in his mind now. "It hasn't been anything against you," he said. "I want to thank you for passing me. I thought maybe you'd give me a bad mark, for giving you such a rough time of it."

"Why should I? You deserved to pass. You have the beginnings of a fine talent. If you treat it right, if you study and work, there's no telling how far you'll be able to go."

"I've read your book," said Markham suddenly. "I liked it."

"Thank you. Now, what did you really think of it?"

Markham smiled suddenly, and visibly relaxed. "I like you, Mister Blake," he said. "You're all right. And I really did like the book. It got kind of awkward sometimes, but most of the time it was fine."

"That's a strange thing," said Blake. "When I wrote it, I didn't care if it was any good or not. I just felt like writing it. Do you know what I mean?"

"Sure. That's the same feeling I get."

"I've tried writing books since then. They didn't work out, because I wanted them to be good." Blake grinned. "That isn't exactly what I mean."

"I know what you mean," said Markham. "You know, those two stories I sold, I didn't think much of either of them, really. Not really. I have some others I like a heck of a lot better, and they'll never sell to anybody."

"Then why did you write them?"

"Because I felt like it."

There was silence for a moment, and Blake broke it. "What did you really want to talk about, Dave?" he asked. "It wasn't my book, or the mark I gave you. It was something else. What?"

"Janice," said Markham. The one word flattened in the room, leaving silence behind it, and Markham stood up into the silence and turned his back. He walked across the living room, pacing carefully, watching his feet as he paced, and turned at the end of the room to pace slowly back again.

Blake waited for him, and he knew that he had been waiting for him, for Markham or somebody, for somebody to come along like this, ever since that first night when Janice had come here and read him that story and they had gone to bed together. And now the somebody had come, Markham, and Blake was surprised to discover that he felt nothing but relief. Markham had turned away again, still pacing, still staring at the carpet, and Blake said, "What about her?"

"I love her." Markham stopped. He looked at Blake, his eyes weak and blinking behind the lenses of his spectacles, his acne-spotted face only comic, with its expression of tragedy. "She doesn't know it," he said. "She wouldn't look at me twice anyway." He turned away, gesturing wildly. "I don't know why I came here," he said. "I was going to confront you or something, I don't know. Tell you about Janice, what kind of girl she really is, make you stop seeing her—It wouldn't make any difference. If it isn't you, it'll be somebody else. I made a mistake. I shouldn't have come here, it doesn't matter whether you know about her or not."

"Know *what* about her?"

"Nothing, it's nothing." Markham was edging toward the door, shuffling nervously and wiping his hands constantly against his sides. "Look, I'm sorry I came, it doesn't mean a thing, I don't know anything about Janice anyway. And it's only puppy love or something. Look, I'm going to drop out of the class, all right? I mean, I'm just a nuisance and an annoyance anyway, I might just as well drop out. And I won't come around on Friday nights any more, either."

"Listen, Dave, don't be silly—"

"It isn't silly. I just annoy everybody, and I know it, and I can't help it. So I'll just drop out and stay away and let it go at that." He had reached the doorway by now, and he stopped for a second, his hand on the doorknob. "It isn't your fault, Mister Blake, it's just the way I am," he said. "And I don't really know anything about Janice, anyway, that was just a lot of nonsense. And I'm not really in love with her, that's just talk, it doesn't matter if she comes here every night or not—"

"She doesn't," Blake told him. "Not any more. I think you're talking to the wrong man. I think you got here too late."

Markham looked blank. "Then who?" he asked. "Who else? I thought it was you."

"It used to be," said Blake. "For a while. But it isn't anymore. At least, not completely. She still comes around, every once in a while." He turned away, reaching for his cigarettes. "I'm not sure she's found somebody else yet, maybe she's just looking now, but it's ending. I've known it for a couple of weeks."

"You'll know when she's found somebody," Markham told him. "And it won't take her long. When she's found a new one, she'll stop seeing you completely."

Blake lit his cigarette, looked over at Markham. "Now," he said, "while she's looking, why don't *you* do something? Tell her how you feel. Maybe it would work out."

Markham shook his head. "I don't think so. She despises me, like everybody else. I've just got a lousy personality, that's all. Maybe I'll grow out of it someday, or smarten up or something." He pulled open the door. "I'm sorry I bothered you," he said. "I'm sorry I came here, I didn't really have anything to say. I won't come around any more."

"Dave—" said Blake, but Markham had gone out, pushing the door shut behind him, and Blake heard Markham's footsteps rushing down the stairs, and then the sound of the outer door slamming.

Janice came the next night, Friday night, when the regular discussion group met. Dave Markham was absent again, and Blake spent the evening studying Janice, wondering about her, wondering whether she had found the new man yet or not, wondering what she had been looking for in him.

When they made love that night, he knew it was the last time. She was cold and unresponsive. She smiled at him when he spoke to her, but it was a faraway smile, a distracted smile, and he knew she was thinking about someone else. He touched her breasts, the red-brown nipples, but they stayed loose and flat in his fingers. He caressed her legs and her belly, fondled her breasts, but she lay unmoving, uncaring, passive. He touched her with his lips and his tongue, her breasts, nipping the insides of her legs with his teeth, pinching her buttocks, stroking her, rubbing himself against her, and she smiled at him without moving, not caring what he did to her, not responding to him.

In a sudden frenzy, he fell with her, loving her brutally, harshly, bitterly, and at last she responded, moving sluggishly. He bit her neck and her earlobe, pulled her hair, pinched her nipples, and she clawed back at him. He punched her, bit her, squeezed her, trying to hurt her, and she slowly came to life, fighting back against him, moving with him, and then she shuddered, and whispered, "Blake!" and from then on it was good. He made it last, he went slowly to make it last, and she lashed his back with his nails, crying, "Faster, faster, dear God, faster!" But he went slowly, and he forced her to move slowly too, to make it last, because he knew it was the last time.

10

IT WAS A LONG WEEK. He knew it was over, that Janice had either found someone else or was even now looking for someone else, but he tried not to believe it, and he knew he wouldn't have to believe it until the following Friday. On Friday, she would come to the meeting. If she stayed, then everything was all right. If she left with the others, then it was all over. He knew it was finished anyway, but still he spent the week doubting, hoping he was wrong, hoping she was still his, for just a little while longer. He didn't want anything permanent with her, but he did want her to stay with him at least until the school year had ended.

He got his answer on Friday. He got more of an answer than he had expected. Janice didn't come to the meeting at all. And neither did Greg Matheson. He couldn't understand it for a few minutes, didn't connect the absence of the one with the absence of the other, and then he saw it. Greg Matheson, the tall, bearded, adventurous intellectual, the perfect combination of the physical and the mental. Of course Janice would be interested in him. Of course she would turn to him when she realized at last that what she was seeking she wouldn't be able to find with Blake. Of course he would take her, and of course he would disappoint her.

And he had brought them together. He grinned sourly at himself as he thought of it. He had invited Greg Matheson to these meetings, he had then been quiet, had sat quietly to one side, while Greg took over the role he had held in the discussions, while Greg took over his girl.

He didn't blame Matheson. Matheson probably didn't even know that there had been anything going on between Blake and Janice. So far as Blake knew, Matheson had lived an ascetic life since he had come to Monequois College, and a girl like Janice was tough to resist.

Without the perception of Matheson, the argumentativeness of Dave Markham, the presence of Janice, the meeting was dull and lifeless and boring, and Blake spent most of his time in the kitchen, fooling with the coffee pot and trying to figure out what to do next. It was barely March. There were three months of the spring semester yet to get through, and then he was free. Free for what? He had saved no money, had made no plans, had no idea what he planned to do in June. The students left, at last, and Blake sat in the darkened living room, a bottle of vodka on the floor beside his chair, and for the first time since the beginning of the school year, he got very drunk and slept sitting up in the living room.

Annette came to see him Saturday afternoon. He was hung over and dull feeling, and was sitting at the kitchen table reading freshman themes when the doorbell rang. A faint hope stirred that it might be Janice, but he knew better than that, and he plodded through the apartment to the front door, pressing the door-release buzzer as he stepped outside to the outer hall and the staircase.

He didn't recognize her at first. She was dressed conservatively, almost severely, in a dark gray suit and a white blouse with lace fluff at the collar, and her hair was tied back in a stringy pony tail. She came up the stairs slowly, as though tired, and when she reached the top, she looked at him with surprise. "You're Blake?" she asked him, as though she thought she had made a mistake.

Then he remembered her. "Yes," he said coldly. "I'm Blake. What do you want?"

"I want to talk to you," he said. "I've got to talk to you." She sounded almost hysterical, as though she had been steeling herself for some terrible ordeal and now she wasn't sure whether she could go through with it or not.

He stepped back, giving her room to pass him. "Come on in," he said.

"Thank you."

He followed her into the living room, closing the door behind him. He kept trying to figure out what she was doing here. Was she wondering why he hadn't come back again, had she thought he was going to be a steady customer? Or had she—and the cabdriver, too, probably—realized that there was the possibility for some small scale blackmail, because of his position at the college? He remembered the cabdriver then, and his conviction at the time that the cabby was watching all the time he had been with this girl—and then he remembered her name. Annette, yes, Annette. "Sit down, Annette," he said, motioning at the sofa. "Go on, sit down."

She perched nervously on the edge of the sofa, her hands fidgeting in her lap, her face seeming ever paler and thinner than he had remembered. He stood looking at her, waiting for her to say something, and when it became obvious that she wasn't going to speak until spoken to, he said, "Well? What is it? What did you want?"

Then she spoke. "Janice loves me," she said, in such a small and weak voice that it took a minute for the sense of what she had said to register on his mind. In that minute, with her first three words still ringing in the air, she stared boldly up at him, defying him. "She loves me," she repeated. "I don't care what she's promised you, or what you've promised her, or what you've done together or what you've said together, it's me that she loves, me, me, and I'm not going to give her up, I'm not going to, I'm not, I'll never give her up." And she was crying.

Blake stared at her, a kaleidoscope of thoughts and half thoughts racing through his mind, trying to fit what this girl had said into the reality he knew, and the only coherent thought that came out of the jumble was the realization that she was crying, this poor whore was crying, and he ought to do something to console her. He took a step toward her, his one hand extended as he said, "Annette."

She shrank away from him, glaring up at him through her tears. "I'm not going to give her up," she said. "She loves me, she does, she's only afraid of what people would think, that's all. But it doesn't matter what people think. We're in love and that's all that matters. We'll go away together, I've saved my money. She doesn't need you, she doesn't love you, she loves me."

"Wait a second," he said. He sat down in the nearest chair, staring at her. "What is this? Janice? You're in love with Janice?"

"And she's in love with me," said Annette. "I know she is. Here, here, I can prove it." She had a large, plain black purse with her, and now she rummaged through it, finally emerging with a letter, a crumpled and obviously much-read letter, which she passed across for Blake to read.

He took the letter from the envelope and opened it. It was Janice's handwriting, he saw that right away, he knew her writing well enough by now from all the assignments she had handed in. She used the typewriter only for final copies. He smoothed the creases from the letter, resting it on his knee and rubbing his palm across it, straightening it out, stalling until the last possible moment before he began to read.

The letter began, "Darling Annette," and said that they, Janice and Annette, would have to stay away from one another for a while, that Janice's father was suspicious, that one of the boys who had caught them together out at the old road had been a boy from the neighborhood. It closed with assurances of unfaded love, and ended, "All my love, Janice."

The old road. Now he knew how it was that Janice had happened to pick that road, on that day when they had gone off together to talk, to decide their affair, to make love and wash themselves in the icy water of that stream. Janice had been there before. She had been there before, with Annette.

Silently, he put the letter back into its envelope, and handed it to Annette. "I didn't know," he said. "She didn't tell me about you."

"Do you believe me now?" she asked him. She held the letter triumphantly in her hand and her eyes blazed at him.

"Do you believe me now? Now, will you let her go? She isn't yours, she doesn't love you. She's mine, she loves me."

He shook his head. "I'm afraid you're too late, Annette," he said. "There's nothing I can do now. Janice has already left me. She left me over a week ago."

"Left you?" Annette was staring at him, not understanding, not believing.

"Over a week ago," he told her. "It's been more than a week since she's been here. She left me, just as she left you, without saying that she was leaving."

"She wouldn't leave me!" flared Annette. "She'd never leave me, she loves me, she's in love with me—"

He got to his feet. He didn't want this pitiful little whore in the house any longer, he didn't want to have to look at her or talk to her any longer. He wanted to be alone, he wanted to have some time to himself. "I can't help you," he said. "If I could give Janice up, I would, but I can't, because she gave me up first. So I'm afraid I can't help you. And I'm afraid I can't sympathize with you either. I think the best thing for you to do is leave."

"But—If it isn't you, then who is it?"

"I don't know," he lied. He didn't know why he was keeping this knowledge from Matheson, why he was saving Matheson from an interview like this. He spoke instinctively, and left the contemplation of the act for later.

Annette got to her feet, a frail, thin, pathetic creature, wearing dignity like an ill-fitting robe. "Janice is going to come away with me," she said, as though she believed it herself. "That's why she left you, because she's going to come away with me now. I'm sorry I disturbed you. I didn't know that things were all right now. Thank you for talking with me."

"It was perfectly all right," he said. He walked her to the door and stood at the head of the stairs, watching her as she made her dignified retreat. Once the downstairs door had closed behind her, he returned to the living room and sat down to try to think.

Janice. Now she was with Matheson. Before that, she had been with him, Blake. And before that, she had been with the whore, Annette. A lesbian. No, worse than a lesbian, if that were possible. A parasite, a sexual parasite, and it didn't matter to her whether her host were male or female. Blake felt unclean, all at once, as though he had suddenly been flung headlong into a full garbage can.

For the first time in weeks, he thought of Ann. He remembered the first few weeks they had spent together, and now they seemed good to him. There had been none of the fire, none of the excitement he had had with Janice, but there had been no foul aftertaste either. And he had given it up. For what? For a pig, a beast, a woman who was worse than a whore, worse than a queer.

He wondered if it would do any good to go to Ann again, to apologize and try to explain. He'd never be able to explain to her, he knew that. He couldn't really explain it to himself. But he could apologize to her, if he could talk to her—that was all he asked for now. He didn't ask for the relationship to start again, all he asked was for her to listen to him, to talk to him.

He got to his feet and walked through the apartment to the back door. He walked across the echoing wood floor of the back porch, and hesitated by Ann's door. A streak of light in the space beneath the door told him that she was home. Nervously, he tapped on the door.

She opened the door at once, as though she had known he was standing there, as though she had only been waiting for him to knock. She glared stonily at him and held the door open only a few inches. "What do you want?"

"Ann," he said. "I wanted to talk to you."

"What about?"

"I—I wanted to apologize, Ann, for the way I acted—"

"Accepted," she said, and slammed the door in his face.

And the slamming of the door woke him up. What the hell was he doing here, apologizing to Ann? For what, for not having married her? He was feeling sorry for himself, that was all. He'd been conned by an oversexed little pervert, and he was feeling sorry for himself. That didn't mean he had to go crawling around on his hands and knees for the rest of his life. He went back to his own apartment, carried the vodka bottle into the living room, and drank himself to sleep.

The next week was a haze. School was becoming more remote, less real, less meaningful to him. He was behind in the grading of freshman themes, but it no longer seemed important to grade freshman themes. He was distracted and unaware in class, and he spent every evening alone in his apartment, drinking and remembering the good time, the year he had written that first book, and what a good time that had been.

And why couldn't he write another one? What was it that kept him from writing another book? Good Christ, he'd had less when he wrote the first book than he did now. He was older now, he knew more, he was aware of more. He had a couple of hundred dollars in the bank now. When he'd written the first book, he'd been broke, he'd been absolutely broke. One or two days a week, he had gone to work for some Office Temporary organization, earning just enough to buy his food and pay his rent and keep him in paper and typewriter ribbons. And he had written a book, he had written a hell of a fine book. So why couldn't he write one now?

He brooded about it all week, and Friday night, after the writing group had left the apartment, he hunted through the apartment until he found the copy of his first book. He sat in the living room, the vodka bottle standing on the floor just to the left of the chair, and he stared for a long while at the cover of the book. Then he began to read.

The vodka made him sleepy, and he only managed to read half the book that night. He finished it Saturday afternoon, and when he had finished it, he sat for a long while, thinking about what he had read.

It wasn't what he had meant. This was the first time he had looked at the novel in three years, and he suddenly, for the first time, saw that he hadn't written what he had meant, he hadn't said it right at all. Oh, the damn thing was fairly competent, it was good enough from a twenty-four-year-old, but it wasn't what he had meant to say at all. From the viewpoint of what he had meant to say, it was terrible.

Now, he realized the way he should have said it, the kind of characters, the kind of background and plot that would have brought it out, would have really brought it out. Not this thing, this *Drink Deep The Night*. God, what a sappy title! And to think he had once been proud of that title.

Without realizing it, he was on his feet. He had to try again. The hell with agents or publishers or anybody else. He didn't care if he never wrote a salable word again as long as he lived. That wasn't the point. The point was that he hadn't *said* it right, and now he thought he could say it better.

The opening was clear in his mind. He hurried into the bedroom and took the portable typewriter out of its case. As he set it on the desk, he heard a faint tapping at the kitchen door. Now, who the hell was that? It didn't matter who it was, he had the first sentence clear in his mind, the first paragraph—

The tapping came again, and with it a voice, Ann's voice, calling, "Dan? Dan?"

He couldn't do it here, he couldn't write the book here. There was Ann, there was Freshman English, there was the goddam writing class coming by every Friday night. He wouldn't be able to get anything done here, not in a million years.

So the hell with it. The hell with it all. They could sue him if they wanted to, he was through, he was finished. He put the portable typewriter back into its carrying case, and opened his closet door, searching for the suitcase. He didn't find it where he had thought he had left it, and decided the hell with that too. He didn't have anything worth taking with him, anyway. He went into the bathroom, grabbed his toothbrush and razor, the latter in its plastic case, and shoved them both into his trouser pockets.

Back in the bedroom, he shrugged into his coat, picked up his typewriter, and headed for the front door. Ann was still rapping at the back door, still calling, "Dan! Dan!"

He ran down the stairs and climbed behind the wheel of his Ford. He drove out to the highway and turned from Winston, toward New York. He stamped his foot down on the accelerator and the car raced ahead, roaring and complaining as it tore down the highway.

Forty miles from the college, the car broke down, and he hitch-hiked the rest of the way.

EPILOGUE

IT WAS SIX-THIRTY IN THE EVENING, and raining, when he came across the George Washington Bridge. The driver was a printer's supplies salesman, a round, balding, affable man who liked to talk. He had two topics of conversation, selling and sex, and he never slowed down with either of them. Blake nodded from time to time, as though he were listening, and stared out through the rain at the feeble lights of the city. The doubts had started ten miles from Winston, and had grown stronger with every additional mile. He had run out on his contract. Why? He couldn't think of a sensible answer.

The salesman was asking him a question. "Excuse me?"

"I say, where do you want to get off?"

"Anywhere. It doesn't matter."

"I can take you downtown a ways. I'm staying at the Manhattan. Eighth Avenue and Forty-Fifth Street."

"Okay. I'll get off there."

It didn't matter where he got off. It didn't matter where he went. There was nothing waiting for him. Nobody waiting for him. He stared out at the rain and the million feeble lights, and he cursed himself for an idiot.

The affable salesman, still talking, hugged the right-hand lane across the bridge, slipped left to the lane for the Henry Hudson Parkway, and they were rolling south, the river dark on their right, the city a choppy dim-lit cliff to their left. The salesman was driving a new Plymouth—"Company car, and I'm beatin' the hell out of it!"—and the street-number exits ticked off, until they reached the Forty-Sixth Street exit, and the salesman braked smoothly as they came down the ramp. They had to wait for a red light, and Blake said, "I guess I'll get out here. Thanks for the ride."

"Sure thing," said the salesman.

Blake walked along Forty-Sixth Street. It was cold and damp, with a steady drizzle of rain, and the typewriter was heavy. Cabs, with the vacancy light glowing on their tops, passed him, headed for Times Square.

At Ninth Avenue, he walked up a block to Forty-Seventh. He seemed to remember some cheap hotels along Forty-Seventh, between Eight and Ninth. They were still there, tenement buildings calling themselves hotels, with wooden signs beside the entrances, reading, "Transient-Permanent-Private Bath." He walked into the first one he came to, and a sloppy middle-aged fat woman traded him key for money and told him where he could find his room.

His room was on the third floor, and he climbed the dim stairs and the halls smelling of the exterminator. The exterminator wasn't very successful, apparently. When Blake entered his room and flicked on the light, there was a rustle and a scurry, and he stood watching the cockroaches running along the walls and out of sight.

He put his typewriter down and glared at the room. This is what he left Winston for. He was an idiot, that was all, an idiot. A super-colossal idiot. He remembered the book, and his thinking that he hadn't succeeded in that book, hadn't said what he wanted to say in the way he wanted to say it. So what had he thought he was going to do? Rewrite a three-year-old book which had already been published?

The room was small, with bare walls that had once been painted yellow. Faded and cracked linoleum covered the floor, and his private bath was a closet containing a filthy toilet and filthier shower stall. The furniture was only one step above that found in a prison cell. There was a dresser, a scarred and sagging relic. There was a brown kitchen chair, with two rungs missing from the back. There was a throw run on the floor, the nap almost completely gone. And there was a bed.

Blake walked across the room to the bed and threw back the covers, to see if the sheets were clean. The fold creases and the lack of wrinkles testified that the sheets were fresh. The flurry of cockroaches racing for cover testified that they were not clean.

He couldn't stay here, not now. He'd come back later on, pull the bed away from the wall, maybe he could get some sleep. Tomorrow, he'd move. He'd sign up with one of the outfits that hired temporary office people. He'd get a decent room somewhere. And he'd try to figure out what the hell he was doing here in New York.

But right now, he had to get out of this room. He hurried back down to the first floor and said to the woman who had rented him the room, "Do you want to spray some roach powder around in my room? I'm going out for a while now."

"If there's any roaches up there," she told him, "you brought them in with you."

"All those? I couldn't carry that many cockroaches if I had a truck. Spread some poison around, okay?"

"I'll see if Luther ain't busy," she said.

"Good girl."

He left the building and walked uncertainly through the rain for a while. The streets were full of rushing cabs, but the sidewalks were almost deserted. A row of bars fronted by neon signs promised warmth, and a hiding place from the rain. He walked into one of them, and stood just inside the door, taking off his sopping coat and looking at the place. It was a long narrow room, split in two, from side to side by a waist-high iron railing. Behind the railing was the dining room, now empty. In front of the railing was the bar, along the left-hand wall, and a few unoccupied booths to the right.

There were seven people at the bar, all being served by a no-longer-young barmaid, a woman fantastically fat, whose breasts loomed halfway across the black surface of the bar-top. Four of the customers were Puerto Rican whores, tightly sheathed in too-bright dresses, their faces looking like cartoon strip characters, with the long curving line of re-drawn eyebrow, the black-mascaraed and black-lined eyes, the creaseless and heavily made up skin, the longbow mouth, their bodies young and smooth and hard. There were three men at the bar, one of them a sleeping sailor, one an angry looking cigar smoker in a blue double-breasted suit, and one an unhappy husband in gray flannel. One of the whores was with the sleeping sailor, buying herself drinks with his money. The other three clustered together in the middle of the bar, laughing and chattering in Spanish.

Blake debated. The bar? No, he was tired, he needed to lean his back against something. He sat down at one of the booths, and waited, wondering if the fat barmaid would desert her post to serve him.

She didn't. She poked one of the whores, gestured toward Blake, and rattled off a stream of Spanish. The whore came over, her hips undulating, and smiled as she said, "Yes, sir?" Her accent was soft and fluid, and her eyes, surrounded by the childish makeup, were a clear and liquid brown.

He ordered beer, and she swayed away from him again. She wore a fitted dress, black, with the silver line of the zipper showing down her back, from her neck to her rounded, rolling buttocks. Blake looked away from her and lit a cigarette. He couldn't afford it even if he wanted it.

She came back with the beer and said, "Here you are, sir. Anything else?"

"Sorry," he said. "We could talk, maybe, but otherwise I'm broke."

"Would you like to talk?" she asked him.

"Of course."

She shrugged. "It's a slow night, because of the rain," she said, and slid into the seat across from him.

"Can I buy you something to drink?"

"No, I'm all right."

"I'll have some money soon," he told her. "I just got back to the city tonight."

"You were away?"

"Yes. In Limbo."

She smiled, and he noticed the cross dangling from a chain around her neck. Limbo is for the unbaptized," she said.

"And for those who have lost their faith. Tomorrow, I am going to start writing a book."

"A book? What about?"

"Me. And you. Do you sometimes give credit?"

Her smile was pleasant, and honest. "I don't always charge," she said. "I am a very poor businesswoman."

"My room is full of roaches," he told her.

"So is mine," she said. "We might as well go to yours."

"I'll throw you out tomorrow. I have to start on my book."

"I will bring you coffee. And sometimes doughnuts."

They got up from the booth, and one of the other whores called over in Spanish. Blake glanced from one to the other. "What did she say?"

"That I am crazy." The whore smiled again, and shrugged, and he helped her on with the coat. Then they walked through the rain to the hotel.

Also on Blackbird . . .

KEPT	Sheldon Lord
YOUNG AND INNOCENT	Edwin West
ELIZABETH TAYLOR	John B. Allan
SHABBY STREET	Orrie Hitt
THE DEVIL SPEAKS HUNGARIAN	Seth Edgarde

Check out our other great titles at:

BLACKBIRD BOOKS
www.bbirdbooks.com

www.ingramcontent.com/pod-product-compliance
Lightning Source LLC
Chambersburg PA
CBHW051257250626

47155CB00009B/3323